LOVE'S DAWNING

Rosanne Charlton joins her friend Ruth and family for a holiday in Southern Ireland. Unfortunately, the holiday is marred for her by the arrival of Ruth's brother, Brendan O'Neill, whom Rosanne has always disliked. However, Brendan's presence is not Rosanne's only problem . . . Trouble and danger close round her, like an Irish mist, when she becomes unwittingly involved in mysterious activities in the bay — and finds herself fighting for survival in the dark waters of the Atlantic.

DINEY DELANCEY

LOVE'S DAWNING

Complete and Unabridged

LINFORD
Leicester

First published in Great Britain in 1982 by
Robert Hale Limited
London

First Linford Edition
published 2006
by arrangement with
Robert Hale Limited
London

British Library CIP Data

Delancey, Diney
  Love's dawning.—Large print ed.—
Linford romance library
1. Love stories
2. Large type books
I. Title
823.9'14 [F]

ISBN 1–84617–449–X

Published by
F. A. Thorpe (Publishing)
Anstey, Leicestershire

Set by Words & Graphics Ltd.
Anstey, Leicestershire
Printed and bound in Great Britain by
T. J. International Ltd., Padstow, Cornwall

This book is printed on acid-free paper

For Sheila

1

'Well, what do you think?'

Rosanne Charlton gazed out across the hot, dusty street, crowded with hot, dusty people as she considered her friend Ruth's suggestion. She longed to escape the summer city and it certainly was a tempting offer, a month in Ireland with Ruth and her boisterous family. She knew them all well and was fond of them, but she had commitments at home to be considered. The afternoon sun shone through the dirty window of the café, dappling the tablecloth with dancing shadows. Rosanne studied these for a moment before she glanced back at Ruth's expectant face and smiled.

'Well,' she said, 'I don't know. It sounds a great idea but . . . '

'Come on,' urged Ruth. 'You said yourself you'd got nothing planned for

August, and George is away.'

'I know I did, I know he is.' Rosanne toyed with the teaspoon in the stainless steel sugar bowl as she thought. 'I agree there is nothing specific, but I must get myself prepared for next term. It's not back to the old routine, you know. I've got to have some pretty detailed ideas worked out for this new job, and if I go away for the whole of August it only leaves me a couple of weeks now and one in September to produce them.'

'Go on,' said Ruth. 'You can do it with your eyes shut. And,' she went on persuasively, 'you could always do some work while we're there.'

Rosanne laughed aloud at that. 'What with your noisy lot around?'

Ruth grinned. 'Well, I agree they're not the quietest of children, but they'd love to have you there and so would I. With David away chatting to Arabs in Kuwait, the month in Ireland alone with the children seems to stretch into eternity, but if you were there too . . . ' Her words hung unfinished and there was a moment's silence before Rosanne asked, 'Where is this cottage?'

Sensing her friend was weakening, Ruth put down her cup of tea and, leaning forward, launched eagerly into an excited description of the cottage and its surroundings.

'It's just outside a little fishing village called Kilbannon.'

'Where's that?'

'Right in the middle of the south coast. There are several super beaches nearby — miles of sand and rocks with rock pools, and a little harbour — well, not much more than a jetty really where there are a few small fishing-boats. The country round is lovely too, with hills and lakes and woodland. The gorse and heather'll be out . . . '

'All right, all right,' cried Rosanne, laughing and holding up her hand to stem the flow, 'I'm convinced, I'm convinced.'

'You mean you'll come?'

'I'd love to, it sounds too good to be true.'

'That's marvellous!' Ruth's chubby face was alight with pleasure and she could see her own excitement reflected in Rosanne's more delicate features. Their friendship had blossomed as soon as they had met even though they were very different both physically and in character. Ruth was short and a little dumpy, having had three children in fairly quick succession. Her cheerful face was pink, rounded, framed with unruly dark curls, and her brown eyes were warm and laughing. Rosanne, on the other hand, was tall and slim with a neat firm figure which caused Ruth a pang of envy when it was displayed in a bikini on the beach. She had a determined chin and wide, candid, grey eyes; her fine fair hair was generally knotted loosely with a scarf at the nape of her neck, but she sometimes piled it high on to her head if she felt the occasion demanded something more formal.

In personality, too, they differed; Ruth a little scatty and disorganised even though she managed her lively family with good-natured firmness, Rosanne with definite views about most things and a brisk common sense which stood her in good stead in her professional life. Perhaps it was their humour that drew them together, both had a lively sense of the ridiculous that had seen them safely through their training, teaching practice and life in a two-roomed flat at the back of Battersea. They complemented each other perfectly and faced the idea of sharing a cottage in a small Irish community for a month without any of the qualms which would have beset many people planning such a holiday together.

'David'll be pleased, too,' Ruth said. 'He was a little worried about my having to go on my own, afraid I'd be worn out by the children, even though the cottage has been modernized to a certain extent.'

'Where did you hear of it?' asked Rosanne. 'Have you seen a picture of it?'

'Oh, we've been there before,' said Ruth. 'It's Brendan's.'

'Brendan?'

'Yes, my brother. You remember, you met him once when he came over to see me at college, after he'd finished at Trinity. He had tea with us in the flat.'

Rosanne did indeed remember, but did not tell Ruth just how she recalled the occasion. She remembered it clearly and with little enthusiasm. She considered Brendan O'Neill a domineering, self-opinionated, arrogant man and it was only out of friendship for Ruth that she did not say so to his face at the time. Even now she could visualize him sitting in the dowdy brown-wallpapered sitting-room of the Battersea flat, his dark eyebrows raised quizzically and his lips curved in a disdainful, cynical smile, as she and Ruth and their other flatmate, Anne, had discussed the movement towards a more flexible system of education. The recollection of his attitude nearly ten years ago to his 'little sister' and her friends still

6

irritated Rosanne, but she merely said, 'Yes, of course I remember. A scientist of some sort, isn't he?'

Ruth nodded and laughed, then as if answering Rosanne's unspoken thought said, 'He didn't think much of you either,' and continued before her friend could protest, 'Don't worry, he's mellowed with age. He's had a girlfriend called Mary, who seems to have civilized him a bit. Anyway, he won't be there, he'll be in America at some conference or other, that's why the cottage is free at all. He normally uses it himself in August, but he can't this year, so we're lucky.'

'Well,' admitted Rosanne, 'I must say it's probably a good thing. I'm not at all sure we'd have got on, but it doesn't matter anyway.' She poured them each another cup of tea, selected a large piece of chocolate cake from the dish before them and settled back comfortably in her chair.

'So,' she said, 'Tell me when we go and how we get there.'

Ruth stayed only ten minutes more and then, promising to telephone Rosanne with the final arrangements, whirled off to collect her children from her mother-in-law and David from his office. Rosanne ordered herself another pot of tea and sat back peacefully in the deserted café to consider the decision she had just made. She wondered what George would say and immediately told herself that he would want her to go and enjoy herself.

'After all,' she reasoned, 'he's off on some Greek island somewhere, burrowing in the ground, unearthing priceless relics.' At least that was how he had described his archaeological holiday. 'So there's nothing and no one to hold me here, provided I get next term's work organized.' And yet she felt almost as if she were sneaking off behind George's back, accepting Ruth's invitation without talking to him first. 'That's ridiculous,' she said aloud. 'He didn't discuss his holiday plans with me.'

'Beg pardon, dear?' said the surprised

waitress, looking up from the magazine she was reading in a corner.

'Oh, nothing, sorry,' murmured Rosanne and flushing with sudden embarrassment at being caught talking to herself she picked up the teapot and poured herself a cup of tea which she did not really want.

The trouble with George was she never knew just where she stood with him. Sometimes he was considerate and affectionate, others he was distant, even offhand. He was unfailingly cheerful, almost too much, for he was never serious about things which might cause him concern, and though he was obviously fond of Rosanne and found her good company, he never committed himself or allowed his feelings for her to interfere with his other plans. Rosanne knew this and had accepted it as the way George was; in a way it suited her, too, as she was not sure of her own feelings, but occasionally it struck a spark of irritation, and recalling the jaunty way he had announced, 'I'm off to Greece on Sunday,' a few weeks ago, she found that anger arising inside her again now.

'Serve him right to come back and find I've gone,' she thought; for she had missed him more than she had expected in so many little ways and she knew in her heart that he was not missing her. 'A complete change is what I need,' she told herself firmly. 'And Ireland with Ruth will be just the thing. I can't imagine anyone brooding with her, Michael, Clare and Julie about.' And so with her decision confirmed, she dismissed George firmly to the back of her mind, where he belonged, and stepped out into the warmth of the summer afternoon, a pleasant glow of anticipation within her.

In the days that followed, Rosanne worked tirelessly, preparing herself for the next term so that she could go to Ireland with nothing hanging over her to cloud her holiday. She had just landed herself a new job in the History Department of a big comprehensive school and was determined to show well there; not only did she have the responsibility for all the history taught in the first and second years, but she also had pastoral care of a large group of children. Rosanne always enjoyed her work, finding it easy to establish a good working relationship with children; this was mostly because she respected them as she required them to respect her. She had discovered that if she gave serious consideration to views expressed by the children she worked with, they in turn were ready to attend to her and discuss ideas and situations arising both in and out of the classroom. This attitude, coupled with her readiness to see the funny side of things and a strong streak of common sense, led her to succeed in her chosen profession and, though her life did not consist entirely of school and its attendant problems, they formed a great part of it, particularly in term-time, and she found she was really looking forward to leaving it all behind for a month of relaxation and freedom from responsibility.

Her preparations for the next term led her to the local library and while she was there she paused a moment to search out books on Ireland and its history, especially those relating to the area where she was going. As always, little snippets of the local history caught at her imagination and she found she had several books to take with her by the time she came to pack her suitcase.

She considered writing to George and telling him about Ireland, but as so far she had received only one hastily scrawled postcard since he had left nearly two months ago in reply to her steady stream of letters, she hardened her resolve to forget him until he came home again, and found it easier now that she had definite plans to make.

'Let him wonder what's happened to me,' she thought viciously. 'Let him wonder and worry.' And once again she pushed him firmly to the recesses of her mind, determined to keep him there until her Irish holiday was over.

'I'm really looking forward to this,' she told Ruth as she scrambled into the car to begin the long drive to Pembroke Dock. 'I feel like a child again.' Ruth grinned back at her.

'I know just how you feel.' She jerked her head towards the confused noise in the back of the car. 'We've all got a touch of holiday fever.' She raised her voice to make herself heard above the hubbub.

'Come on, everyone,' she cried, turning to the three excited children bouncing on the back seat, 'Let's go to Ireland!'

2

'Ah, 'tis a fine soft Irish morning,' laughed Ruth, her gentle Irish lilt becoming suddenly more pronounced as she scented the cool, damp morning air of her home. She eased the car from the stifling car-deck of the ferry and immediately had to switch on the windscreen wipers as thin drizzle hung like a misty curtain from leaden skies. Rosanne laughed, too, and in a fair imitation of her friend's accent said, 'It is indeed! A grand morning,' and helplessly laughing and with the children joining in, they sailed through customs and out into the grey morning streets of a Cork city barely awake, and then on, following an almost empty road, westwards.

They passed through small towns, with blinds and curtains still drawn against the night; huddled villages with colour-washed houses crouching along the road; besides rivers, water tumbling over stones or gliding smoothly between banks of leaning trees, until they reached the coast once more.

'Are we nearly there?' asked little Julie, the youngest of the three children. She had been asking the same question at regular intervals ever since they had driven off the boat train and Ruth's voice was a little sharp as she replied, 'Not very far now, but don't keep asking, darling, because it doesn't make us go any quicker.'

Rosanne was entranced by the countryside, which had changed gradually from smooth green fields patchworked to the horizon, clumps of trees and whitewashed farms dotted among them, to sharp outcrops of rock, jutting grey and hard amidst the promised purple and gold of heather and gorse; but she realized that the journey had been tedious for the children, who longed to arrive, so she started a game with them.

'The first one to see a cow!'

'There, over there!' cried Michael at once, pointing to two black and white cows grazing a patch of roadside grass.

'Well done,' said Rosanne. 'A point to you. Now, the first one to see a tractor.' The game progressed quickly, with Rosanne keeping score, and suddenly Ruth joined in. 'The first one to see a sign for Kilbannon!' Michael soon spotted one and Ruth swung the car off the main road and followed the narrow lanes which led across the hills to emerge at last overlooking the sea.

'The sea! The sea!' cried all the children, pressing their noses against the car windows, and bouncing up and down with excitement. It was indeed, and Rosanne felt a bubble of excitement inside her, too, as she looked out over the smooth blue expanse of water spread before her. The thin drizzling mist had gone, and the sun, pale silver as it probed and pierced the web of cloud above, struck sparks of brilliance from the restless water.

'It really is a grand Irish morning,' she breathed and continued to peer from the window as avidly as the children. The car nosed its way down the steep hill towards the village sheltering in an inlet, protected by a jutting headland from the huge Atlantic rollers which so often pounded the shore. Just before they reached the village Ruth took another lane and drove about two hundred yards before swinging through an open gate into the garden of a small white cottage and sliding to a halt beneath a canopy of fuchsia.

The children exploded from the car and rushed round the tiny garden, looking at everything to see if it was all as they had remembered. Ruth leaned back in the driving-seat for a moment before starting to unpack the car, glad they had arrived safely and suddenly exhausted by the drive. Rosanne got out of the car and stretched her legs, also pleased to have arrived and eager to see where.

The cottage was a small two-storey building with gabled windows jutting from under blue slates. Two squat chimneys perched on the roof and the rough and slightly bulging walls had been newly whitewashed. It seemed to doze in the morning sun sheltered by its high fuchsia hedges on three sides and a stone wall giving on to a steep track on the fourth. Rosanne took deep breaths of the warm clear air and could smell the tang of salt upon the breeze. Listening, she could hear the rhythmic movement of the sea, no more than a gentle sighing in the wind, and for one extended minute she was lapped in the peace and beauty of that Irish cottage garden and she felt, in some indescribable way, renewed. The worries and burdens of her new job and George dropped quietly away from her, acquiring a new perspective, and she found herself smiling with pure joy as she stood there in that moment, breathing in her new surroundings.

Momentary it was, shattered immediately by the return of the excited children demanding to be let inside, and Ruth climbed out of the car to open the door for them.

'Come on, Rosy,' cried Clare, the middle one. 'I'll show you everything,' and Rosanne went in willingly, to be shown the cottage from the inside. It was not as small as it had appeared from the garden. Clare dragged her from room to room, pointing out the things that pleased her.

'We have lovely peat fires here,' she cried, pointing to a large open grate in the living-room, 'and there's the gas bottle for the cooker.' She flung open a cupboard in the little kitchen to reveal the yellow cylinder of gas. 'And this is where we keep our boots and buckets and spades,' she cried, rushing on to show Rosanne a small back porch with another door leading into the garden. Almost before Rosanne had had time to admire, the child caught hold of her hand again and dragged her up the steep narrow staircase which led to the bedrooms.

'This is our room,' she said, pushing open a door to show a small bedroom lit by one of the gable windows Rosanne had noticed from the outside. There were two sets of bunk beds and a chest of drawers. Michael had already claimed one of the top bunks and was unrolling his sleeping-bag on it to maintain possession.

'I'm having the other top bunk,' announced Clare and abandoning the guided tour clambered hurriedly up on to the bunk. There was a wail from Julie, who had just appeared at the door carrying her sleeping-bag to stake her claim.

'I wanted to be up there!'

'Well, you can't,' stated Clare firmly. 'You're much too small, you'd probably fall out.' Julie began to protest at the top of her voice, but was cut short by Ruth, who had arrived puffing at the top of the stairs.

'Don't worry, love, everyone can take

it in turns. Clare, you and Michael help me carry things in. Julie, show Rosy her room, she's in the end one.' Julie, who had calmed down immediately she heard she could have a turn in the top bunk, said cheerfully, 'OK, come on, Rosy,' and taking Rosanne by the hand led her to the second room with the gable window. This was also furnished very simply, with two divans, a chest of drawers, a small hanging cupboard and rush matting on the floor. It was already warm from the sun and Rosanne crossed to open the window. From it she found she could see out over the thick fuchsia hedge across a meadow which sloped away to a cliff, to the sea beyond. Again for a moment she was captured, spellbound by the beauty around her and then, with a tug at her sleeve, Julie brought her sharply back to the present and they hurried downstairs to help unload the car.

For the next hour everything was in chaos, but gradually things began to be sorted and were found places to live.

Ruth took the car down to Kilbannon village to collect the groceries she had ordered in advance, leaving Rosanne and the children to finish unpacking and restore some kind of order. While she was exploring the kitchen Rosanne found a tall glass jar and it struck her how pretty it would be with some sprays of fuchsia in it. She found some kitchen scissors and slipped out of the back door into the garden. She snipped several of the twigs laden with bursting red flowers and then, before carrying them indoors, paused for a moment to lean over the wall and look up the farm-track to see where it went. Up above the cottage on the hillside was a clump of trees screening a large white house. Its roof and chimneys were well above the trees and it was clearly at least three storeys high.

'The view from that house must be fantastic,' thought Rosanne. 'I wonder who lives there.' Even at that distance it looked deserted and she wondered if it was another holiday home. She was just turning back to the cottage when she heard a car coming up the lane. Thinking it was Ruth, Rosanne went round to the front of the cottage to meet her. It was not, however, Ruth's car which swung in at the gate but a battered grey Ford with Irish number plates. Surprised, Rosanne went forward to see who had come, still clutching the boughs of fuchsia in her arms and smiling as the car door opened and the driver got out.

He had aged little since Rosanne had last seen him, his hair was still thick and dark, and from under brows still raised in that quizzical manner which had so irritated her before he gazed at Rosanne with an unrecognizing stare. The smile of welcome died on her lips and she took an involuntary step back. For a moment neither of them spoke and then the strange, awkward silence was broken by the three children, who came rushing out of the house.

'Uncle Brendan! Uncle Brendan! What are you doing here?'

It was a question Rosanne had wanted to ask herself and she listened now to his reply as he fended off the children as if they were boisterous puppies.

'Down! Down all of you! Why shouldn't I be here — it's my cottage. Where is your mother?' And then ignoring the chorus of excited replies he turned his attention once again to Rosanne.

'I see you've been cutting the hedge,' he said and then continued smoothly before she was able to reply, 'Where is Mrs Merton? Is she not here?'

Rosanne at last gathered her wits about her, and staring straight back at Brendan O'Neill, said lightly, 'She's down in the village, collecting groceries. Will you come in and wait for her?'

'Come in? Of course I'm coming in. You can make me some coffee.' He turned abruptly to the children. 'Off you go, kids, go and play.' Dumbfounded at the tone he used to her, Rosanne thought, 'He hasn't a clue who

I am, he thinks I'm the mother's help or something.' She drew herself up stiffly and was pleased to be able to say, 'I'm afraid I can't, there isn't any coffee until Ruth gets back.'

'In the cupboard,' he said shortly and, striding past her, went into the kitchen and from a cupboard which Rosanne had not yet investigated produced coffee, sugar and powdered milk.

'Can I have a drink and a biscuit?' piped Julie, catching sight of a square tin and a bottle of squash also on one of the shelves.

'Yes, love, I should think so,' said Rosanne and, ignoring Brendan's request for coffee, crossed the kitchen to mix up some orange squash. Brendan shrugged, filled the kettle himself and put it on the stove. Rosanne watched him surreptitiously as he stared out of the kitchen window, waiting for the water to boil. Ruth said he had mellowed, but Rosanne could see no traces of it in his face. His lips were compressed into a firm, straight line and his chin jutted determinedly, as determinedly as Rosanne's own, though she did not recognize the fact.

He glanced round and caught her studying him, which caused him once more to raise an enquiring eyebrow, and to her mortification Rosanne felt the colour run hot to her cheeks, like a child caught spying. He left her to her confusion for a moment before he said, 'I'm Brendan O'Neill, Ruth's brother.'

'I know,' replied Rosanne shortly. 'We've met before.'

This time it was Brendan who seemed slightly disconcerted, but only for a moment.

'Have we?' He sounded indifferent. 'I'm afraid I don't remember.'

'No,' agreed Rosanne. 'It was a long time ago.'

As the kettle began to shrill there was the sound of a car pulling into the drive, and Ruth appeared struggling with a huge box of groceries. She nearly dropped it as she saw her brother in the kitchen and hastily dumping it on the table, rushed to hug him, pouring out questions without waiting to hear his replies. Brendan seemed equally pleased to see her and for a moment with their mutual pleasure reflected in their faces Rosanne could see a strong family resemblance which she had not noticed before; the cheerful endearing grin she knew so well in Ruth appeared on Brendan's face, quite different from his usual contemptuous smile, transforming him from a glowering, harsh-featured man into Ruth's attractive older brother, a lovable member of the family.

'You remember Rosanne, don't you?' cried Ruth with a vague wave of her arm towards her friend. 'Flatmate in Battersea. You met her there.'

'Of course,' replied Brendan smoothly. 'I knew her face of course, but couldn't remember the name,' and his smile challenged Rosanne, daring her to contradict him and start a row. Ruth, knowing her brother as she did, grinned happily. 'I don't believe you remember her at all, but, anyway, here she is, Rosanne Charlton.' Brendan solmenly shook Rosanne's hand and said with a gleam in his eye, 'How nice to meet you again, Rosanne. I'm sure we shall be good friends.' Though still irritated by his arrogance, Rosanne found she was laughing in spite of herself, and was rewarded with a fleeting smile.

'Now, Brendan,' said Ruth, who had switched off the shrieking kettle and made three mugs of coffee, 'what on earth are you doing here? You're supposed to be in America.'

'Yes, I know, but I got a call yesterday to say the conference had been postponed.'

'Postponed?' said Ruth. 'Why?'

'Well, believe it or not, the conference centre burned down.'

'I don't believe it,' replied Ruth shortly. 'Burned down? How? You're making it up!'

'No, I'm not! I don't know how, but it burned down, so I thought as David

28

was away I'd come down to the cottage and keep you company.' He glanced at Rosanne. 'I didn't realize you'd brought company with you.'

'You mean you'll stay in the cottage?'

'Yes, of course, it's my cottage, you know.'

'I know, idiot, but where will you sleep?'

'Well,' said Brendan thoughtfully, 'one of us will have to share with Rosanne, and I think until she and I are better acquainted it had better be you, don't you?'

Ruth laughed. 'All right,' she said equably. 'You don't mind, Rosy, do you?'

'No, not at all,' said Rosanne hastily. 'How long are you going to be here, Brendan?'

'Trying to lose me already?' he asked. 'Well, on and off for the whole month. I may have to go back to Cork for the odd day or two, but I expect you'll survive without me.' He crossed to the door. 'That's settled, then. I'll get my luggage from the car,' he said and disappeared.

'Well,' exclaimed Ruth and laughed, 'he'll be quite fun to have, really. Don't look so thunderstruck, Rosy, he won't be here all the time and you might even get to like him!'

Rosanne was not so sure, but she kept her doubts to herself, for she was determined to enjoy her holiday and would not allow people like Brendan O'Neill to interfere with that, so she smiled and said, 'Of course I will, I can see he's great fun.'

3

'Well, what are we going to do today?' asked Ruth next morning as they sat comfortably over a second cup of coffee at the breakfast table.

'I want to go to the beach with the rock-pools,' cried Michael. 'I'm going to catch some fish.'

'To Sandy Strand,' said Clare. 'Let's go to Sandy Strand, we can build castles there.' Julie bounced up and down, chanting, 'I want an ice-cream. I want an ice-cream.' Ruth's voice rose above the clamour. 'One at a time, one at a time. We've plenty of time to do it all even if it's not all today.' There were more cries of excitement and argument until Brendan, who had been gazing peacefully out of the window, turned round and without raising his voice quelled them all.

'Go into the garden, all of you. Your

mother will decide what we are going to do.' There were subdued murmurs of 'Yes, Uncle Brendan,' and Rosanne heard Clare mutter to Michael, 'Come on, he's got his cross face on.' Rosanne glanced up at him and saw he had indeed got his 'cross face' on. The harsh lines had returned to the corners of his mouth and his eyes, sometimes bright with laughter, were diamond-hard, their soft brown turned almost black.

'Don't be too hard on them, Brendan,' said Ruth, 'they're only excited.'

'Possibly,' said Brendan, 'but there's no need to turn the breakfast table to a shambles.' His voice brooked no argument and Ruth shrugged slightly before turning to Rosanne.

'Well, it's a lovely day so I suggest we take a picnic lunch somewhere.'

'If you go to Kilbannon Strand,' said Brendan, 'you'll have rock-pools and sand.'

'Good idea,' said Ruth, while Rosanne thought, 'For all his jumping on the children he did bother to listen to what they wanted.'

It was a successful day; the first of several. The weather, so often damp and misty, had settled fair and the sun shone down from a windless sky, warming Rosanne through to the very core so that she felt relaxed and comfortable, like a cat basking in the sun. They passed the days on the strand, playing football and cricket, digging castles and extensive fortifications for the sea to wash away, and allowing the slow-moving tempo of the days to penetrate gently until they lost all sense of time and Rosanne was hard put to say which day of the week it was.

Occasionally when everyone was settled on the beach or in the evening when the children were in bed and Ruth was recovering from the day aided by a large gin-and-tonic, Rosanne would borrow the car and slip away on her own. She loved exploring the countryside, seeking out the remains of the castles which had once guarded the coasts and protected the families of the large landowners. Often she would stop at a farm near to one of these and talk with the farmer or his wife and hear the legends and tales linked with the ruins. She discovered circles of standing stones, grey and ageless as they kept their silent vigil and, pausing among them, she felt a strange sense of awe at their age and the thread of continuity running between those who had lovingly raised them, and herself now standing amidst them. It was a feeling she was unable to put into words and so when Ruth asked where she had been Rosanne simply said, 'Oh, exploring the country, looking at local history,' yet in another way she longed to share the closeness with the past such places gave her with someone who would understand. If only George were here. The thought was on her before she realized and yet after serious consideration she decided it was not he who would understand, and unconsciously she moved another pace away from him.

'I wonder if your George is having such beautiful weather as this,' remarked Ruth one afternoon as they lay back on the sand surrounded by the debris of a picnic lunch. Brendan, who had taken to joining them for lunch each day on the strand while maintaining a comfortable distance from the children the rest of the time, turned lazily to glance at Rosanne, who replied, 'Well, it certainly won't be as peaceful as this.'

'Who's your George?' he enquired with a faint emphasis on 'your'.

'Oh, just a friend,' answered Rosanne, not really wishing to elaborate. George was too difficult a friend to define at the best of times and Rosanne had an underlying feeling that Brendan would have very little time for him and she was reluctant to expose George to his scathing tongue. Then remembering something Ruth had said she added, 'Like your Mary.' What prompted her to this remark Rosanne had no clue, but the moment she spoke she wished the words unsaid. They were greeted by a tangible silence which hung about them like a mist, separating yet enclosing the three of them. Sounds came from the outside, the children laughing as they played leap-frog and the waves tumbling on the sand and creaming round the rocks which flanked the beach. Rosanne felt the colour flood to her cheeks as Brendan said softly, 'Yes, like my Mary,' and Ruth said quickly and brightly, 'Come on, Rosy, you haven't been in the sea yet today.'

The moment dissolved and was gone and, eager to escape Brendan's brooding eye, Rosanne jumped up to follow Ruth into the sea. When she looked back up the beach Rosanne saw the rugs where they had been sitting were empty and Brendan had disappeared. They ran back to their towels warming in the sun and when they had dried and were stretched out once more Ruth said, 'Sorry, Rosy, I should have warned you, only I didn't think that the subject would arise. Mary's just got engaged to someone else. Brendan's not really the marrying kind and I suppose she got tired of waiting. He hasn't said much, but I think he was fairly cut up about it.'

'I see. I'm sorry I put my foot in it, it's just that when he asked about George . . . '

'Don't worry,' grinned Ruth. 'It'll teach him not to be nosy.' But the damage was done and the uneasy truce which had been growing between Rosanne and Brendan returned to its original state of guarded hostility, and the evenings when all three sat together after the children were in bed were tense and awkward. Brendan went fishing several nights, not coming back till it was almost full darkness and while he was out Rosanne and Ruth enjoyed their usual easy companionship, but when he returned Rosanne felt out of place and often went up to read her book in bed, pleading tiredness brought on by the days spent out of doors.

It was on an evening when Brendan was fishing that Paul Hennessy first dropped in. Rosanne and Ruth were relaxing in the late sun outside the living-room window, sharing a bottle of beer and enjoying the peace left by three children safe in bed, when he walked up the track beside the stone wall. Glancing in he saw the two women and raised a hand in greeting.

'Hallo,' he said, pausing to lean on the wall. 'You're Ruth, aren't you? Brendan's sister? We met once before. I'm Paul Hennessy, I live up at Inchmore House.' He waved his hand vaguely in the direction of the white house on the hill that Rosanne had noticed on the first day.

'Of course, how nice to meet you again,' said Ruth, jumping to her feet. 'This is my friend, Rosanne Charlton. We were just having a beer, do come and join us.'

'That sounds grand,' said Paul Hennessy and swung himself over the wall. 'Brendan not about?'

38

'No, he's fishing up at the lake. We're hoping for trout for dinner,' replied Ruth, and she disappeared indoors to find more beer and another glass.

Paul Hennessy eased himself down on to the grass beside Rosanne and said, 'Is this your first visit to Ireland?'

'Yes,' replied Rosanne with enthusiasm, 'and I really love it. It's so beautiful round here.'

'It is indeed,' agreed Paul, 'my wife and I love it down here too. Unfortunately, we aren't here nearly enough, most of the time I'm in Dublin or London. But we keep the house for the few weeks we can come.'

'Is your wife here too?' asked Ruth, appearing round the corner of the house with a tray.

'No, she couldn't come this time.'

They sat chatting as the sun slid down behind the hills and the conversation flowed as easily as if they were all old friends. Paul was naturally charming, and Rosanne found herself warming to him. He was an attractive man with pale blue eyes laughing from a bronzed face. His dark hair was greying at the temples, giving him a distinguished air without betraying age. Rosanne could see him as a successful businessman, always immaculately dressed; even now on holiday his open-necked shirt and cord trousers looked as if he had put them on only the moment before and Rosanne was suddenly conscious of her own T-shirt and faded jeans.

He told them about his house and the picture gallery he had made there.

'It's only small,' he said, 'but I have one or two quite valuable paintings, and I hope it will grow. You must come up some time. I like people to enjoy my treasures with me.'

As the dusk faded into darkness Brendan arrived home, carrying two brown trout. He greeted Paul distantly and disappeared into the kitchen to clean his fish. Paul said his farewells and, climbing back over the wall, continued on up the stony track.

'What did he want?' asked Brendan when Rosanne and Ruth joined him in the kitchen.

'Nothing in particular, why?' asked Ruth.

'I don't like him,' said Brendan.

'Why ever not?' said Rosanne in surprise. 'I thought he was charming.'

Brendan gave a tight smile. 'I expect he can be, when he wants to,' was all he said and Rosanne felt stung by this to retort, 'Perhaps he greets rudeness with rudeness.'

'Perhaps,' said Brendan mildly. 'But I haven't found he improves on acquaintance. I don't encourage him to drop in,' and returning his full attention to his fish, Brendan made it clear he considered the subject of Paul Hennessy closed.

The next afternoon Michael, Clare and Rosanne went on a very successful rock-pooling expedition. Armed with shrimping-nets and two buckets, they scrambled over the rocks at low tide to explore the pools left by the receding

41

water. Some of them were quite deep and glowed with colour, beautiful underwater gardens. The slight movement of the water set the seaweed swaying, pink and grey, green and red in a stately formation dance. Tiny fish darted, flashes of silver, from place to place, and little green crabs scuttled sideways to the shelter of overhanging ledges of rock when the children trailed their fingers in the water. Clare dabbled her net in the pools, but her uncertain swishes merely served to scare all the sea creatures from the open water to the safety of the crevices and sheltering weed, so she took to collecting shells and coloured stones. Michael, however, was far more patient and would insinuate his net into the clear water, causing scarcely a ripple, then he would wait rock-still until one of the darting sand-eels or blennies actually swam into the folds of his net before he jerked it upward, trapping his prey with an expert flick of his wrist. Both children were entirely happy and kept their finds safely in the buckets to display with pride to Ruth when they got back. At last the pangs of hunger told them it was teatime and so they clambered back across the rocks to the beach and, finding Ruth and Julie had already left the strand, they all trailed back up the lane to the cottage, carefully carrying their buckets. They showed them to an admiring Ruth and then left them in the back porch to show to Uncle Brendan when he came in from his walk. Unfortunately, he came in through the back way and as he swung the door open he caught his foot on Michael's pail, knocking it over and slipping on its contents, which had spread across the floor.

'Who the hell left buckets of water in the back porch?' His roar carried clearly to every corner of the cottage, and they all converged on the kitchen to discover the damage.

'My blennies!' cried Michael in dismay. 'You've knocked over my blennies.' And he scrabbled about on the floor, trying in vain to retrieve his catch.

'They took him all afternoon to catch,' said Clare solemnly accusing, 'and now they'll die.' Brendan got down on his knees on the wet floor to help Michael and managed to pick up two gasping blennies.

'Sorry, old chap,' he said, his own temper evaporating as he saw the disappointment on Michael's face. 'I didn't know the bucket was there.'

Michael, in a slightly strangled voice said, 'It's all right, Uncle Brendan, I can catch some more.'

'Of course you can,' Brendan agreed. 'Indeed you will, tomorrow afternoon. I'll take you round to the end of the rocks to some pools I know. We should find some whoppers there.' Michael's miserable face was transformed as he beamed at his uncle.

'Will you? Will you really, tomorrow?'

'I will,' affirmed Brendan, getting up and wiping his wet hands on his already damp trousers.

'Can I come too?' cried Clare, catching hold of his hand and swinging on his arm. 'Will you take me too — I'm a good climber, Uncle Brendan, can I come?' Brendan considered for a moment and then with a twinkle in his eye he nodded. Immediately Julie was clamouring to go as well, but here Brendan drew the line.

'Not this time, Julie; when you're a bigger girl.' Julie began to wail her disappointment and Ruth tried to comfort her while the two older children cavorted their delight up the stairs to their bedroom. Suddenly the telephone shrilled and shocked everyone into silence. Brendan answered it while Ruth hustled Julie up to bed as well. Rosanne busied herself washing a lettuce in the kitchen, but it was almost impossible not to hear what Brendan was saying in the hallway by the kitchen door.

'Yes, of course I'll come . . . at once. Where are you?' There was a pause and then he said, 'Don't worry, Mary, I'll leave at once and be with you in about an hour.'

Within ten minutes he had thrown a few things into a grip and was out of the house, saying briefly to Ruth, 'I've got to go to Cork. I'll be back as soon as I can.' And with no further explanation he was gone.

4

Michael and Clare were devastated when they found Brendan was missing from the breakfast table next morning.

'But where's he gone?' cried Michael. 'When's he coming back?'

'He said he'd take us fishing,' moaned Clare. 'He promised. He said he'd take us right round to the end of the rocks to some big pools.' Ruth tried to soothe them, saying she was sure he would take them when he came back.

'Uncle Brendan doesn't forget his promises, you know. Don't worry.'

'But when's he coming back?' asked Michael again.

'I don't know, darling, but soon, I expect. In a day or two.'

'That's no good,' muttered Clare mutinously. 'It'll be too late then.'

'Don't be so silly, Clare,' said her

mother sharply. 'The pools won't go away.'

Rosanne felt sorry for them and, hoping to overcome their disappointment a little, said, 'I tell you what, if it's still sunny this afternoon I'll take you round the rocks.' The children's faces brightened considerably at this.

'To the very end?' asked Michael.

'Where the big pools are?' said Clare.

'Yes,' promised Rosanne. 'To the very place Uncle Brendan would have taken you.' Ruth looked a little doubtful.

'It's quite a scramble, Rosy, do you think you can cope?'

'Yes, of course,' said Rosanne. 'I like rock-climbing.'

'I know, but some of the rocks out there are pretty high, you know, with steep sides, it's not quite like the ones round the beach.'

'Don't worry,' said Rosanne reassuringly, 'I promise we won't tackle anything we can't manage.'

And so it was that, with some misgiving, Ruth waved off the two children and Rosanne, armed with bucket and shrimping net, on their journey of exploration across the rocks and then settled down to build sandcastles on the strand with Julie.

It was a perfect afternoon with hot sunshine and the faintest breath of breeze to temper the heat. The tide was ebbing fast, leaving gleaming patches of sand tucked amongst the tumbled rocks. The scramble out to the end of the little headland was not difficult and the children climbed confidently without any help from Rosanne. Several beautiful rock-pools, bright with their miniature gardens and mirror still, caused the children to stop and exclaim in delight, but it was the promise of the wide deep pools described by Brendan that led them on further from the safety of the strand, towards the final jagged teeth standing black in the swirling tide. Michael went on ahead, picking out a route across the walls of rock which barred their way. Between these were narrow gulleys, floored with smooth clean sand. They had steep rocky sides making natural corridors from the cliff-face to the sea. He scrambled up one of these and balancing on the ridge at the top waved excitedly to Clare and Rosanne, following his trail.

'Here they are! There are two enormous pools here,' and he jumped down to investigate his find. Rosanne and Clare were soon beside him and all three lay down on a large flat rock above the first pool and peered into its depths. It was alive with tiny fishes and transparent shrimps almost invisible until they moved.

Michael started stalking with his net at once while Clare crossed the sandy strip between the rocks to the second pool on the opposite side.

'There's a cave here too,' pointed out Rosanne and for a moment they left the pools to peep inside, but it was dark, dank and smelt of decaying seaweed and they soon returned to the warmth of the sun and the fresh air.

'Don't go off this little beach, you

two,' called Rosanne, and with their promises to stay in sight she sat down on a smooth, flat rock, and with her back against another shut her eyes to enjoy the peace and the sun. The waves pounded the ends of the rocky corridors and the steady rhythm of the sound soon lulled Rosanne into a comfortable doze; sheltered from the wind and warmed by the sun she drifted away into untroubled sleep while the two children crawled round the two rock-pools with nets adding to a rapidly increasing collection of sea creatures in their bucket.

It was Clare who noticed the change first; crouching with her back to the sea, leaning over and flapping with her hands to encourage a reluctant sand eel into the toils of Michael's net, she was suddenly drenched with cold spray. With a cry of surprise she jumped up and looking behind her found the sea was level with her rocky ledge, the swirling foam receding towards the next incoming wave only to be gathered up and flung forward once more, this time not as high but inching its way up the sandy-floored passageway between the rocks.

'Michael!' she cried in alarm. 'Michael, the sea's coming. Michael, who had stripped off his shorts and shirt and was now sitting on a flat rock in the middle of the pool, looked up.

'What?' he said. 'What's the matter?'

'The sea's come in,' said Clare. 'I've just got wet.'

'Well, we'll wake Rosy in a minute,' said Michael. 'But there's a crab down there, I just saw him go into a crack by my feet. I'm going to try and prod him out.' Clare stood and watched excitedly as he poked the handle of his fishing-net down a crevice in the rocks. For several minutes they probed, watching hopefully for some sign of the hidden crab, but they were suddenly reminded of the sea by another huge wave actually breaking over the rocky wall and swishing into the stillness of the pool.

'You're right,' agreed Michael reluctantly, and waded across the pool to collect his clothes before they were soaked by the water.

'Rosy,' he called as he jumped down on to the few yards of sandy beach not yet covered by the tide. 'Rosy, we ought to be going back, the tide must have turned.'

Rosanne woke with a jerk and looked in cold horror at the waves rushing up between the rocks, encroaching a little more on the sand each time.

'You're right,' she said, leaping to her feet. 'Come on, we must get back at once, as quickly as we can.' She glanced at her watch; they had been out among the rocks for two hours. Ruth would be worrying if they were not back soon. She did not want to frighten the children, but she urged them on as much as she could, carrying the precious bucket and nets herself so that they could climb unhindered. Before they had gone twenty-five yards Rosanne realized they were in real trouble; the rocky corridors to the sea were all of different lengths and depths, and as they crested one ridge they found their way forward blocked by a surging tide of water, sucking greedily at the rocks and gurgling noisily as it struggled amongst the nooks and crevices in the rock-faces.

'Stay here,' she warned the two children, and clinging to the spiny ridge, she lowered herself into the heaving water below. Her feet did not touch the bottom and the water pulled eagerly at her legs, dragging her body away from the rock. She hung on grimly, with her fingers hooked over a little ledge, and as the water slackened, hauled herself clear of its grasp and struggled up on to the rock once more.

'We can't cross there,' Rosanne said to the two white-faced children, who had now begun to realize their danger. She looked at the cliff carefully to see if there was any hope of climbing up out of reach of the water, but the face rose sheer from the rocks, like the smooth trunk of a tree from a jumble of exposed roots. There was no escape that way.

'I'm afraid we've been cut off by the tide,' she told the children, forcing herself to speak calmly and quietly to hide the rising panic within her. 'We can't go on this way and I think the water covers these rocks at high water, so we can't stay here either.'

'What above the cave?' suggested Michael. 'Perhaps we'd be safe in there.'

'Good idea,' Rosanne said bracingly. 'We've got to go back that way anyway, so we'll have another look at it. Come on let's go.'

As they retraced their route back across the rocks towards the tiny inlet where they had spent the afternoon, Rosanne's eyes kept searching the blank face of the towering grey cliffs, hoping to find a ledge or crevice that might afford them some sort of safety above the high-water mark, but there were none and every minute the sea seemed to close in on them, forcing them towards the smooth wall of the cliff. When they reached the little beach they found it almost covered; only five or six yards of sand were still exposed and the waves licked round the rock-pools reclaiming them once more. Rosanne and the children jumped down on the shrinking oasis of sand.

'You two wait here.' Rosanne spoke a little harshly in her fear. 'You are not, repeat not, to move. I'm going to look into the next inlet. Michael, look after Clare. Don't worry, I'll be back in a minute. We'll probably be able to get round this way instead.' She sounded more hopeful than she felt and managed a brave smile as she left them waiting on the diminishing beach and clambered up the rocks on the other side of the beach to see what lay beyond. Almost at once Rosanne knew it was hopeless. Again she was faced by a deep gorge already filled with the oncoming tide.

'If I were alone,' she thought, 'I might

make it, but the children will never get across, and if by some miracle they did struggle to the safety of the next rocky ridge, they would be faced with many more such crossings each becoming more dangerous as the tide continued to rise.' She hurried back to the two children now cowering at the gaping mouth of the cave they had seen earlier.

'Well, I'm afraid we'll have to brave the darkness of the cave, chaps,' Rosanne spoke cheerfully. 'I expect smugglers used to use it to hide their goods, don't you?'

Clare, who up until now had maintained a pale-faced silence suddenly burst into tears and cried, 'I want to go home. I want my mummy.' Rosanne dropped to her knees and enveloped the little girl in her arms.

'You will go home, darling, just as soon as the tide starts to go out again. We'll go into the cave away from the water and then find Mummy when the sea's gone down again.' She turned to Michael, whose bottom lip was beginning to judder as he saw his sister's tears.

'Now, Michael, you're the man of the party, you take one of Clare's hands and I'll take the other and we'll find somewhere to wait.' But, as they entered the gloom of the cave Rosanne's heart sank. The sandy floor was damp all the way to the back wall, and there was a slimy line around the rocks, showing where the water came up to, and that line was too high.

'Come on, we must explore,' she cried. 'Clare, where do you think we might sit?' Keeping her voice cheerful, Rosanne made a quick tour of the cave and as her eyes grew used to the dimness she found she could pick out a jutting unevenness at the back. There, a large piece of rock leant away from the back wall, making a breakwater for the waves to buffet but affording little shelter. Michael, a little braver now that he, too, had got used to the half-light, felt his way all round the walls and on reaching the mouth of the cave again a cry which echoed eerily in the gloom.

'Rosy, Clare, come quickly, I've found a dry ledge.' They rushed over to him and found him standing on a piece of rock beside the cave's entrance. He was reaching above his head and Rosanne climbed up beside him to see what he had found. She felt relief surge through her as she ran her hand along a ledge about two foot wide, broadening a little at one end to make a flat shelf. It was above the high-water mark, and the rock, though cold, seemed dry to the touch.

'Well done, darling,' she breathed and turned to Clare, who was standing patiently below her. 'Give me your hands, Clare, and I'll hoist you up.' Rosanne clutched the child's hands and hauled her up to the rock where she was standing, then heaving her upwards managed to tip her on to the narrow ledge.

'Move to your left, love, where it's wider and sit quite still.' There was a shuffling noise as Clare did as she was told and then Rosanne said, 'Are you safe?'

'Yes,' came back the tiny reply.

'Good girl. Hold tight, here comes Michael.' He was much heavier, but using Rosanne as a sort of ladder he managed to climb up on to the shelf beside Clare. Rosanne looked down and saw the first gleams of frothy water edging on through the mouth of the cave, and reaching up with her hands, hauled herself upwards, scrabbling with her sandalled feet against the rock-face in her efforts to climb up. At last she heaved herself on to the ledge and sat puffing with her legs dangling down over the edge.

They sat, trapped, on the narrow ledge above the entrance of the cave for three hours. The sea rushed in below them and the sound of it echoed and boomed in the confined space until their heads spun with the noise. Even so, Clare fell into an uneasy sleep, her head lolling against Rosanne's shoulder, and Rosanne sat with her arm tightly round the little girl, terrified that she would slip into the surging water. To pass the time Rosanne and Michael played games and told stories, and when Clare woke, stiff and frightened, they all sang songs, their voices raised in defiance against the continuous pounding of the sea. Rosanne knew their ledge was safe above the water-line, but she was afraid that when the sea had filled the mouth of the cave there would be no more air and they might suffocate. How long did it take for three people to use up an air-pocket in a small cave? She had no idea, and determined not to add to the children's fears, she prayed silently within herself that she would be able to return Ruth her children unharmed by their adventure.

At last, after an eternity of fear, Rosanne could tell that the sea was going down and when once more she could see the gleam of the wet sandy floor in the dim light which penetrated from outside, she climbed stiffly down and peered out into the grey evening outside. The sun had gone, the clouds were gathering and a general greyness blanketed the world.

'Come on,' she called, turning back into the cave to help the children descend from their refuge. 'We can't go yet, but it won't be long before the water's low enough. It comes in very fast so let's hope it goes out equally fast.'

They were all glad to be out of the dim dark cave and shivered from the cold of it. Rosanne felt particularly chilled as she had been wet to the waist in her attempts to cross the inlet earlier. They waited on the gradually lengthening beach and Rosanne made them do physical jerks to get warm again. Although the sun had disappeared, the air was not cold and when they had run and jumped and swung their arms for a few minutes, they felt warmer.

'We'll give it five minutes more,' said Rosanne, consulting her watch, 'and then we'll start back. With luck the water should be low enough all the way then.' But before they began their trek back they heard the sound of a motor-boat cruising slowly outside the line of rocks and then as it drew nearer heard someone with a loud-hailer calling, calling their names.

'Michael! Clare! Are you there? Rosanne! Rosanne!'

'It's Uncle Brendan!' cried Clare, leaping in the air and waving both arms over her head. 'It's Uncle Brendan!'

They all called and waved and Rosanne thought, 'I feel as if I'd been marooned for years,' as with infinite relief she saw Brendan carefully nosing his boat into the wide mouth on the inlet and at last beaching it on the sand. The children rushed to him, shouting unintelligibly what had happened, and he gathered them into his arms, soothing Clare's tears which had begun to flow again and hugging Michael, who was battling manfully against tears of his own. Rosanne walked slowly down the beach and met Brendan's eyes above the children's heads. His patent relief at finding them all safe changed to barely controlled anger as he watched her approach and climb into the little boat.

'You stupid, stupid woman,' he spoke softly, his voice was clipped with fury and his eyes were black with rage. 'Talk about irresponsibility! You could all have been drowned. Where the hell have you been? I've been up and down this stretch for hours.'

Rosanne suddenly felt exhausted, she was unable to fight him any more, and desperately close to tears herself, she said tiredly, 'We were in the cave. There was nowhere else,' and she turned away so that he should not see how reaction had already set in and she was shaking.

Brendan lifted the children into the boat and then, skilfully manoeuvring out between the black teeth guarding the inlet, pulled the outboard engine to life and sped them all to the safety of the strand where Ruth was waiting to carry them off to the cottage.

'We'll leave the boat here,' said Brendan. 'Help me drag her up beyond the tide line.' Mechanically Rosanne took her place on the opposite side of the boat and together they hauled it up the beach until it lay on the dry sand by the seawall. Rosanne left Brendan knotting the painter carefully through an iron ring in the wall, and started trudging back towards the cottage. She heard him call, but ignored him. She was in no mood to cross swords with him again. Her anger at the way he had spoken to her lay buried beneath her anger at herself for allowing the frightening events of the afternoon ever to have happened; and, above all, she had to fight against a strange tiredness which made her legs feel like jelly and her feet like lead.

It made her start when Brendan caught up with her and took her arm. He pulled her to a halt, turning her to face him and for a moment he looked down at her so pale and drawn, then he said, 'You look all in.' Rosanne did not reply, but started walking slowly along the lane again. Brendan did not release his hold on her arm and stopping her again said, 'I'm sorry I shouted at you, I shouldn't have, it's just that we were so worried.' Rosanne nodded and said wearily, 'I'm sorry too, it was all my fault, I didn't realize the tide . . . ' Her voice trailed off. She found his brusque kindness brought the hard-fought tears nearer than his anger had and she turned abruptly from him, determined he should not see her weakness.

'Come on,' said Brendan, 'let's get home.' And maintaining a firm but comforting hold on Rosanne's arm, he piloted her back to the cottage.

5

The beautiful weather had broken at last. The grey clouds which had rolled in with the tide the previous day hung low in the sky and damp creeping sea-mist silently enfolded the hills, the cottage, the garden, with clammy fingers, smothering the outside world in a cold, white blanket.

The children, now quite recovered from their ordeal, bounced noisily about the house with new energy and caused Brendan to escape directly after breakfast, saying he would not be home again until late. Rosanne was glad to see him go and breathed a sigh of relief as she heard his car disappear down the lane. Ruth, as quick as always to understand her friend's feelings, said, 'Well, that's him gone for the day.' She glanced across at Rosanne. 'Cheer up, Rosy,' she said encouragingly, 'he'll get over his mood, Brendan never stays angry for long. It's just that I was in a bit of a state when he got back yesterday, and when he couldn't find you either he was as worried and frightened as I was.' Rosanne set down her coffee-cup and looked at her friend, then drawing a deep breath she said, 'Ruth, I really am sorry about yesterday. When I think what might have . . . ' She shuddered. Ruth leant forward and took her hand. 'No permanent damage done,' she said gently. 'I should have warned you about the tide; after all, at least I knew it was tricky round this coast.' She smiled a little tremulously despite her brave words and added, 'And you did keep them safe for me, thank you.' For a moment there was silence as again both of them were conscious of how differently the adventure might have ended; then Ruth said briskly, 'Forest walk today, I think,' and pouring another cup of coffee for each of them she went on, 'we can't stay cooped up with the children here all day or we'll go mad. We'll go for our walk, have lunch at home, then if it's cheered up we'll drive somewhere this afternoon. If not, perhaps we'll go into town and take the children to the pictures.'

Rosanne said, 'I may go down to the village this evening, I saw a poster about an organ recital in the church which I thought might be good.'

'Rather you than me,' laughed Ruth. 'Organ music is not my scene, but you go by all means. I'll be fine here, the kids'll be in bed and I can finish my book in peace.'

Just before they set out into the misty morning there was a tap on the door and Rosanne opened it to find Paul Hennessy standing on the step. He smiled as she greeted him and said, 'Hope I'm not interrupting anything, I just thought you might have a coffee-pot on the go. I've been down to buy a paper in the village.'

'Well, come in,' said Rosanne and stood aside as he strode into the house.

'Ruth,' she called, 'Paul Hennessy is here.' Ruth, who was posting children's feet into the relevant wellington boots in the back porch, appeared, looking harassed.

'Hallo, Paul,' she said, 'we're just on our way out.'

'So I can see,' said Paul watching Julie turning in careful circles, trying to catch the second sleeve of her anorak. 'So I won't stop. I only popped in to say hallo, but I'll get out of your way. Don't forget, though, we must fix a day for you to come up to Inchmore to have a drink. I'd like you to see some of my paintings.' He eased himself out of the house as smoothly as he had eased his way in and as Rosanne closed the door behind him Ruth said, 'Have you noticed he only 'drops in' when Brendan's not here. He knows very well Brendan doesn't like him.' Rosanne was beginning to wonder if she liked him either — there was something altogether too smooth about him — but she said, laughing, 'Sh, he'll hear you, he's hardly out of the door.'

'Don't mind if he does, really,' said Ruth. 'His offer to show you his paintings sounded more like etchings to me.' Rosanne laughed.

'I doubt it, I'm not his type.'

'From what Brendan says all women are his type,' said Ruth drily.

'And he'd know of course,' said Rosanne. Ruth grinned as she heard the asperity in her friend's voice.

'Brendan's no fool,' she said and, turning her attention to her children's outdoor attire, went on, 'Right, you'll do. Into the car, everyone. Don't forget your boots, Rosy. Let's go.'

The forest walk was beautiful. The winding path that led up through the trees was carpeted with pine needles and springy underfoot. Occasionally it broadened into a little clearing where there were rustic seats and promise of a view out over the cliffs to the sea. Today this was wreathed in the shifting mists, but Rosanne was certain it would be breathtaking on a clear day, and determined to come back.

Beside the path under the damp mossy banks were tiny wild cyclamen, glowing pink, luminous in the shadows where they grew.

'Aren't they perfect?' cried Rosanne, kneeling on the wet ground to look more closely. 'I've never seen such delicate flowers.'

'Can I pick some?' asked Clare, crouching down beside her. 'They'd look lovely in a vase.'

'They would,' agreed Rosanne, 'but they look even more lovely here, where they're at home, don't you think?'

Clare looked disappointed. 'Can't I take just one to show Uncle Brendan?' Rosanne reached out and selected one of the little blooms and nipping its stem neatly handed it to Clare. The little girl took it and held it gently against her cheek, then she gave it back and singing out, 'Look after it for me,' dashed off in pursuit of Michael, who had disappeared among the trees, and Rosanne was left holding the dainty flower to keep it safe for Uncle Brendan.

The children all ran on ahead, lurking in the bushes and hiding behind trees to ambush Ruth and Rosanne, and by the time they had followed the track that looped right through the forest back to the car they were all tired and hungry, ready for lunch.

They spent the afternoon looking at the ruins of a castle on a windswept hill and eating an enormous cream tea in a roadside café, then they went back to the warmth of an open fire in the cottage to play Monopoly until bedtime. When at last the children were ready for bed and Rosanne had changed out of her jeans into a neat linen dress, there was no time for her to do more than grab a cup of coffee before setting off to the village to attend the organ recital in the church.

'I'll see you later, Ruth,' she called as she reached for her jacket and opened the front door.

'Do you want the car?' called back Ruth from the kitchen.

'No, thanks. I'm happy to walk. I've got time if I keep moving and it's getting brighter now.'

'Have fun,' said Ruth and Rosanne closed the door behind her, pleased at last to find herself quite alone.

She followed the lane down into the village, pausing occasionally to enjoy the warm damp fragrance of the hedgerows which towered above her on either side. Twisted in amongst the brambles were twines of honeysuckle, vivid orange javelins of montbretia, and umbrellas of fuchsia topped the over-grown wall bursting with red 'dancing ladies'.

'I call them 'red arrows',' Michael had confided to her once. 'The girls call them 'dancing ladies', but I think that's cissy.' Looking at them as she walked down the lane Rosanne thought either name was apt. There was a slight breeze among the leaves now and it dispersed the last clinging vestiges of the sea-mist, which had lingered through the day, driving away enough grey clouds to leave a patch of blue sky out over the sea, and by the time Rosanne had walked the length of the village street to the church perched on a mound above the harbour, golden fingers of sun had pierced the grey and were striking unexpected colour from the cottage gardens.

Inside the church was crowded. Rosanne was surprised to see so many people packed expectantly into the pews. All were smartly dressed for the occasion, which was obviously one of the local social events, and Rosanne was glad she at least looked respectable. Glancing round her she recognized several people she had seen about in the village, and wondering if Paul Hennessy might be there too, she looked more carefully along the rows, but could not see him. She was not sure if she was pleased or sorry. Then the stage whispers which had been echoing through the church ceased and in the waiting silence that followed the organist walked down the church to the organ, seated himself and without introduction began the first piece.

The music soared and fell filling the church with a thunderous tide, sighing softly in the lofty shadows, swelling and fading until it engulfed everything and left Rosanne unaware of anything but its tumultuous beauty. Though it was not a work she knew, it carried her with it as the theme swept forward, leaving her occasionally suspended to admire a delicate cascade or intricate outpouring before sweeping on again until it rose in a final crescendo, and silence exploded once more round her.

There was applause and then more music and this time it was gentler. Rosanne felt more relaxed, allowing the music to flow past her, leaving her mind clear so that she began to notice the movement of light through the church windows, the shifting patterns on the tiled floor, the quiet gathering of evening darkening the vaulted roof above; and a strange peace swept through Rosanne as if she had been clenching her muscles tight and had suddenly released the tension. She felt almost light-headed, euphoric.

The music changed again and, full and solemn, claimed her mind once more, but in a strange way it added to her feeling of well-being. There was an interval but while everyone else chattered excitedly, discussing the programme so far, Rosanne felt quite detached from them all, as if she were invisible or watching them through glass. She paid little attention to what was going on round her, but looked at the church itself, reading the memorial tablets on the walls and the commemorative texts in the stained-glass windows. Someone had switched the lights on and the church was suddenly cosy, intimate, as the yellow lamplight enfolded them all.

The organist returned to his place and the expectant hush waited upon the first gentle trickle of music creeping and growing until once more the flood of exuberant sound filled the church.

The final work was one Rosanne knew well, the Toccata in F by Widor. She had always loved it, finding it a most exhilarating and jubilant piece of music. As it burst upon her now she felt an exhilaration and happiness she had never known before, as if she were on the crest of a wave, on the edge of something magnificent and she sat with her eyes and heart aglow long after the final notes had died away and the people round her were scuffling in the pews, picking up handbags, shuffling hassocks and discussing the recital as they streamed out of the church into the summer darkness.

'Magnificent, wasn't it?' Brendan's voice came softly through to her and she spun round to find him sitting immediately behind her, smiling at her surprise in finding him there; but her happiness persisted and instead of taking the defensive stand to which she had become accustomed when dealing with him, Rosanne found herself reaching out to him so that he was included in the moment and she breathed, 'Yes, magnificent.'

The church was nearly empty as they left it and went out into the warm night. Rosanne allowed Brendan to shepherd her through the churchyard and down towards the harbour.

'Have you eaten?' he asked suddenly and Rosanne admitted she had not.

'Will you join me? I know a place where they do excellent seafood; lobster or king prawns or salmon.'

'That sounds delicious,' said Rosanne and then hesitated. 'But what about Ruth?'

'What about her?'

'Well, she may have kept me something.'

'She hasn't,' said Brendan cheerfully. 'I went to the cottage before I came on to the church. Ruth told me you were here and I said I thought I'd join you. She'll guess we've gone off for a drink. Will you come, please?'

Rosanne laughed, still riding her wave of happiness. 'I feel somehow as if

I were playing truant,' she said. 'All right, I'd love to.'

Brendan helped her into his car and then drove out of the village, following the coast-road round the headland until they came to some imposing gates set into a low white wall. He turned in and drove up the long, curving drive which led to a large Georgian house set well back from the road and protected by tall trees.

Brendan led the way and introduced Rosanne to the owner, Neil O'Connor, who greeted them in the hall, showed them into a little bar himself and served them drinks before hurrying off to see about a table.

'This is an excellent place,' said Brendan. 'Not a vast menu, but everything is always first class.'

Rosanne gazed round the room. The furniture, lovingly polished, gleamed in the lamplight, and walls papered in a dull crimson set off to perfection the black-and-white hunting-prints which hung on one and a huge mirror in a gilded frame on another. The room was as warm and welcoming as a friend's drawing-room and Rosanne felt it at once.

'It looks like somebody's home,' she whispered. 'I thought it was a private house from the outside.'

'It was and is,' replied Brendan. 'But the O'Connors have converted part of it into a restaurant and it is one of the best for miles. In the winter they have a fire here,' he pointed to the wide fireplace which now blazed with dahlias, their petals crimson and pink touched with gold, 'and one in the dining-room. It makes you feel you're eating at a friend's house rather than a restaurant.'

The dining-room had the same charm, but on a grander scale. It was a beautifully proportioned room with long windows almost to the floor along one wall and a fireplace, now filled with a tall vase of dried grasses, set at one end. The tables were small and laid with white linen and gleaming silver.

Two other couples were already dining, and Neil O'Connor showed Rosanne and Brendan to a table by a window open to the scent of the summer garden beyond.

The meal as Brendan had promised was excellent, and Rosanne was amazed at how easily the conversation flowed as they enjoyed smoked chicken, cold lobster and a bottle of light dry white wine. Brendan's usual stiffness and cynicism disappeared and he was at pains to draw Rosanne out as they talked about the music they had just heard, Ireland and its history, Rosanne's exploration of the countryside. Brendan was surprisingly knowledgeable, particularly on local history and related tales of battles and risings, famine and folklore which Rosanne found quite fascinating.

'But I thought you were a scientist, not a historian,' she remarked as he finished a story about one of the castles she had visited, now a lonely ruin beside a tumbling stream.

'Does that preclude an interest in history?' he asked and continued before she could reply. 'You'll find a strong sense of history in many of the Irish, we're part of a very ancient culture that's only recently been allowed to flower again. We're very proud of it.' He told her a little about his job, doing research for a big company with offices in Cork.

'It's always fascinating,' he said, 'particularly the project we're on at the moment. That's why I have to keep going up to Cork, I don't want to miss anything even if I am on holiday. If I'd gone to America as planned I wouldn't have been able to be there at the most exciting time.'

They discussed books and found they had several favourite authors in common and it crossed Rosanne's mind that previously she had found Brendan difficult to talk to and now there seemed to be complete ease between them. Indeed, she was chattering and laughing so readily that she suddenly wondered if the wine she had drunk had gone to her head, and she stopped abruptly.

Brendan said, 'What's the matter?'

Rosanne shook her head and said, 'Nothing.' And unwilling to elaborate said inconsequentially, 'It must be getting very late. Ruth'll wonder where we are.'

'I doubt it,' returned Brendan lightly, 'but if you want to go I'll get the bill.' He raised an enquiring eyebrow at her and she nodded, suddenly shy of him. He was so different this evening as if the music in the church had cast a spell and changed him into a completely different person, and Rosanne felt entirely unnerved by the metamorphosis; this was not the arrogant sardonic man she knew as Brendan O'Neill, it was someone far more, well, she could not be sure what exactly, and though she was enjoying her unexpected evening Rosanne felt as if she had been led into an unsuspected quicksand and she longed to scramble back on to the firm ground, to find the familiar, irritating Brendan waiting there. She also found herself wondering if he had brought Mary here and immediately pulled herself up short, angry that she could be interested in such a matter.

On the way back to the cottage they hardly exchanged a word; a companionable silence had descended between them as the last of the euphoria which had overtaken Rosanne in the church subsided to a comfortable glow. The cottage was in discreet darkness when they arrived and the only pinprick of light in the total blackness gleamed from farther up the hill at Inchmore House, and with sudden recollection that she had looked for Paul Hennessy amongst the concert audience in church, Rosanne found she was glad that it had been Brendan O'Neill she had found instead.

He guided her through the darkness to the front door and as he turned the handle Rosanne said softly, 'Thank you for a lovely evening, Brendan.' He released the handle and gently but firmly put his arms round her, holding her close and still for a moment with his face against his hair before he let her go again, saying lightly, 'It was fun, wasn't it?' And Rosanne hurried indoors and upstairs to her room with the warmth of Brendan's strong arms still about her. As she crept into bed, determined not to wake Ruth, who was already asleep across the room, she had a strange but definite feeling that in some way she had changed and that her whole world was turning slowly but inexorably, upside-down. She felt suddenly incredibly tired and was able to give the matter no further consideration before sleep overtook her.

6

Next morning Rosanne had little time for private reflection either. She was awoken by the sound of Brendan ejecting the children from his bedroom with his accustomed early morning temper and within seconds they were swarming over her own bed and edging under the bedclothes with cold feet. Ruth shooed them away to get dressed and began dressing herself.

'Good concert?' she inquired, glancing across at Rosanne, who lingered a few more moments in the warmth of her bed.

'It was beautiful,' said Rosanne simply. 'I felt quite, well I don't know, uplifted. It's difficult to explain.'

'I know,' Ruth smiled. 'Did you see Brendan? You must have been quite late back.' She spoke casually, without any particular interest, and Rosanne was careful to keep her own voice as disinterested when she said, 'Yes, we met up afterwards and went out for a meal.'

'Did he take you to O'Connors?'

'Yes, it was a lovely meal.'

'It would be. You won't want much breakfast, then.'

Rosanne laughed and got out of bed. 'It's funny but even after that huge meal quite late last night I'm starving!'

'I expect my dear brother feels the same, so I'd better start cooking vast quantities of bacon and eggs.'

Breakfast was interrupted, however, by a heavy knock on the front door. Michael answered it and came rushing back into the kitchen.

'Mummy, Mummy come quickly, it's a policeman.' Ruth hurried to the front door to find Garda Murphy, who lived in the village, waiting on the step.

'Good morning,' he said. 'Mrs Merton, is it not?'

'It is.'

'I'd like to be asking you a few

questions if I may.' He spoke ponderously, as if he had learnt his lines and was afraid to deviate from them.

'Well, we're having breakfast,' said Ruth, 'but you'd better come in.'

Garda Murphy solemnly wiped his feet and, having closed the front door carefully behind him, followed her into the kitchen. The three children eyed him with suppressed excitement as he came through the door.

'Michael, give the Garda your chair,' said Ruth, 'and find the extra stool from the hall.'

Michael did as he was bid, though he was reluctant to miss a word of what the Garda had to say.

Ruth offered him a mug of coffee which he accepted and then said,

'Well, what can I do for you? Get on with your breakfasts, children, Garda Murphy won't mind.'

Garda Murphy gulped his coffee and then looking official, he cleared his throat and said, 'It is about last night,' he paused again.

'What about last night?' asked Ruth.

'Mr Hennessy's house, Inchmore House, was broken into and some of his paintings were stolen.'

'Stolen!' cried Ruth.

'Stolen,' repeated Garda Murphy. 'Cut out of their frames. Frames left hanging, they were, on the wall.'

'How terrible,' said Ruth. 'Do you know who did it?'

'I do not,' answered the policeman.

'And what may I ask has it to do with us?' Brendan's voice came from the doorway, making them all jump as no one had heard him come downstairs. Garda Murphy leapt to his feet almost spilling the remains of his coffee.

'Mr O'Neill, sir, I didn't know you were here. I understood Mrs Merton was in the house.'

'She is,' said Brendan, crossing to the table and pouring himself a cup of coffee, 'but so am I. Now, then, what's all this about?'

'Well, sir, Mr Hennessy's house was burgled last night and we are trying to find out if anyone noticed anything unusual during the evening.'

'I see,' said Brendan. 'Well, I wasn't here and nor was Miss Charlton.' He nodded towards Rosanne, 'What about you, Ruth? Did you notice anything?'

'Well, I don't know. I don't think so. What sort of thing had you in mind?' said Ruth, turning to the Garda.

'Did you hear a car or van go up the track towards the house? Being so close to the corner you might have heard a car turn.' Ruth shook her head.

'Or see lights on up there. They must have had some sort of light to cut round those pictures.'

'I saw a light,' said Rosanne. Everyone turned to look at her and Garda Murphy said, 'I beg your pardon, miss, but I understood Mr O'Neill to say that you were out last evening.'

'It was when we got back,' she answered. 'It was a very dark night and I noticed that the only light to be seen anywhere was up at Inchmore House.'

'And what time would that be?' asked the Garda.

'I don't know really,' said Rosanne, 'I didn't notice what time we got back.'

'Approximately?'

'Approximately one-thirty,' said Brendan.

Ruth raised her eyebrows fractionally but made no comment. Garda Murphy said, 'Are you certain of that time, sir?'

'I am,' answered Brendan firmly. 'We were at the organ recital in the church until about ten-fifteen and then went to eat at O'Connor's. We left there some time after one o'clock so it must have been between quarter and half past one.'

'I see, thank you.' Garda Murphy had jotted a few words into his notebook and then said, 'I think that was probably Mr Hennessy's light you saw. He came home at about half past twelve and discovered the theft.' He paused. 'Anything else?'

There was silence for a moment while everyone thought but no one had any more to add and so the Garda slipped his notebook back into his pocket and said, 'Well, if you do think of anything just give us a ring at the station, ask for me or Sergeant Collins, he's in charge of the case.'

'Tell me,' said Brendan, 'is this the only robbery of its kind locally?'

'No sir, we've had a crop of them lately. Several of the big houses hereabouts. Paintings, jewellery and silver. Not security-conscious, that's the trouble with people round here.' He sighed and then said, 'Well, thank you, Mrs Merton, and don't forget if you do think of something.'

Brendan went with him to the door and Rosanne started frying bacon for him while Ruth buttered toast for Julie.

The children burst into excited chatter.

'Let's hunt for clues,' said Michael. 'I'll be the sergeant.'

'What can I be?' said Clare.

'You can be my man.'

'And me!' cried Julie, determined as

always not to be left out.

'All right,' said Michael magnanimously, 'you can be my other man.'

'Not till you've eaten your toast,' said Ruth firmly. 'Come on, Julie, I've just done this piece specially for you. You two can wait for her,' she added, turning to Michael and Clare, who were sliding out of their seats.

With moans of 'Oh, Mum!' they perched on the edge of their chairs until Julie had crunched her way through her toast and then all three made a dash for the back door.

'Put your boots on,' Ruth called after them. 'And look after Julie.'

'Don't go right up to Inchmore House,' warned Brendan, returning to the kitchen. 'You'll be in the way and Mr Hennessy won't want stray kids around this morning.'

With cries of 'We'll be careful,' the children disappeared into the bright sunshine of the morning, leaving the three adults to finish their breakfast at leisure and discuss the news which

Garda Murphy had brought.

'What I don't understand,' said Rosanne, relaxing with a fresh cup of coffee in her hand, 'is that if the paintings were so valuable why did he keep them up in that remote house at all, why not in his Dublin house?'

'Didn't he have any security for them, burglar alarms or something?' asked Ruth.

Brendan shrugged in answer to both queries.

'I haven't a clue. I've never been invited up to Inchmore House and have no particular wish to go there.'

'But didn't you know he had valuable pictures up there?' asked Rosanne. 'He was quite open about them with us.'

'Of course I knew,' said Brendan, a little abruptly. 'Everyone knew. It's one of the reasons that he irritates me so much. His pride in his collection is because it is valuable, not because it's his, collected by him and loved for its own sake.'

Ruth grinned and Brendan seeing her

smile said, 'You can laugh if you like, but I wonder if he'll reckon what he's lost in financial terms or artistic ones.'

'It's funny he should have been burgled while he's here,' mused Rosanne. 'I mean, if I were the burglar I'd have done his house while it was empty. He told us he hadn't been down here since Easter, they could have had all summer.'

Brendan looked at her speculatively for a moment and then said, 'Interesting point that. Especially as the burglars seem to have been in business for some time.'

'Will you say anything to the police?' asked Ruth. Brendan gave a short laugh. 'No, of course not. What could I say? I can't really see any significance in it myself, nothing to go on. It just seems odd, as Rosanne said. I expect he'll be here today seeking commiseration; thank goodness I shan't have to see him.' Rosanne looked up sharply; she was beginning to get used to Brendan being around even if only in the distance and she was surprised to find the idea of his not being there detracted from her anticipation of the day; but it was Ruth who said, 'Oh, where will you be today?'

'Cork. I've some business to attend to, but I'll be back this evening.'

'Just as long as I know,' said Ruth calmly, 'I can cater for you.'

'Don't worry about me,' said Brendan, 'I'll grab a snack somewhere. I'm hoping to be back in time to go fishing.' He glanced across at Rosanne and said idly, 'Have you ever been out spinning for mackerel, Rosanne?'

She shook her head and he went on casually, 'Come with me tonight if you'd like to, I'll set up a rod for you and you can see if you have any luck.'

Rosanne was tempted, but she said, 'Wouldn't you like to go, Ruth? I'd be delighted to baby-sit if you want to.'

Ruth said, 'No, thanks all the same, Rosy, I don't enjoy fishing much, especially if anyone catches anything.' She shuddered. 'But you go if you like.'

She saw her friend's hesitation and said, 'I'm quite happy on my own, you know. I'll have time to get on with the things that I want to do, which is always pleasant.'

'Well, I would like to go, if you don't mind,' admitted Rosanne, and Brendan said, 'Just weigh it all up and never mind my delicate feelings. Let me know when you've decided.' Ruth gave a shout of laughter. 'Delicate feelings!' she cried. 'That'll be the day, brother mine; but don't worry, Rosy'll be on parade,' and Rosanne with a sneaking suspicion that she was being organized and more than a sneaking suspicion that she did not mind said, 'It sounds lovely, Brendan, thank you,' and then added, 'I don't have to stick a worm on a hook, do I?'

This was greeted by a shout of laughter from both Brendan and Ruth, though neither of them were prepared to enlarge on the subject, then Brendan got up from the table saying, 'Well, Rosanne, I'll see you this evening, and if you'd still like to go, we'll go.' And Rosanne, who was determined not to seem over-enthusiastic though she was beginning to have the feeling that if Brendan suggested flying a kite to the moon she might not have dismissed it as ridiculous, said, 'I'll see how I feel when you're going.' But she already knew.

Soon after Brendan had left, the postman made one of his rare visits to the cottage. The children, having heard the van as it toiled up the lane, met him at the gate, and Clare came running in with the single letter he had brought.

'It's for you, Rosy,' she cried, waving it. 'Can I have the stamps?'

Rosanne was about to say, 'Of course you can,' when she saw the handwriting and realized that the stamps were Greek. The letter was from Greoge. She stared at it and was only recalled to her surroundings by Clare asking again, 'Can I, Rosy? I asked first. Can I have the stamps?' Rosanne nodded absently and said, 'Yes, later on I'll give you the envelope and you can soak them off.' Satisfied with this promise Clare rushed back into the garden to tell Michael of her prize and as Ruth was busy in the kitchen, Rosanne escaped upstairs with her letter.

She had left her address with her neighbour in case of emergency and the neighbour had forwarded one or two letters which had arrived; and here at long last was one from George. She had waited so long for it and yet, strangely, now it had come she was not sure that she was pleased to see it. The ache of George's absence had been forced to the depths of her mind not only by her own will-power, but increasingly by the strength of Brendan's presence, though Rosanne was almost unconscious of this. She stared at the letter for a moment, gazing at the familiar scrawl and the unfamiliar stamps and then with sudden decision, ripped open the envelope. It was typically George, brief and to the point and it left Rosanne's mind in a turmoil.

Dear Ros,

This place is fantastic and we are having a moderately successful dig. Why don't you hop on a plane to Athens? I've got to be there on Thursday 14th and Friday 15th, so I'll pick you up and bring you back out to the island. Cable the above address of your flight number and arrival and I'll be there. You could stay for two or three weeks and collect yourself a suntan before going back to school.

Miss you, but see you soon.
Love George.

7

Rosanne spent most of that day on the beach with Ruth and the children, but her mind was far away. Ruth, who had heard about the letter from Clare, made no reference to it, and left Rosanne to herself as far as she could. Rosanne, in turn, tried to enter into the day as usual but found herself churning George's suggestion round and round in her mind. If only he had bothered to write sooner, she would have jumped at the chance to go, but now she was committed to Ireland; not that she wasn't enjoying herself here, but the thought of being with George on an idyllic Greek island made her heart turn over. Could she leave Ruth, suddenly, in the middle of the holiday? Ruth would understand, Rosanne was sure, after all Ruth had been in love, she still adored her David. If he had sent for Ruth she would have gone, wouldn't she? And, anyway, Rosanne told herself, Ruth wouldn't be left alone with the children, because Brendan would be there. Brendan. It was when the thought of Brendan intruded that Rosanne's excitement died away. She could feel how his dark eyes would bore into her when she told them she was leaving, and knew he would not approve of her going. Not that that matters, she told herself hotly as if already defending her decision to Brendan. 'George said he's missing me and I'm missing him.' 'Are you?' Brendan would say. 'You don't seem to be miserable without him.' Then Rosanne gave herself another shake, of course Brendan would say nothing of the sort; it was nothing to do with him; she didn't need his approval for her actions. George had said, 'Miss you and see you soon.' If she were honest, she felt a trifle irritated that he had taken her acceptance for granted, but that was so like George; he knew she couldn't resist him. She pushed the invitation to the back of her mind and decided to make the final decision the next day. Then she would cable her flight and go from Dublin.

She did not find a suitable moment to break the news to Ruth during the day and so she decided to wait until the children were having their supper and she could get the chance of a quiet word. However, as they walked into the cottage in the late afternoon the telephone was ringing and Ruth answered it; then handing the receiver to Rosanne she said, 'Brendan for you.'

Surprised, Rosanne took the telephone and said, 'Hello, Brendan?'

'Hallo. Yes, I'm sorry, Rosanne, but I shan't be back this evening, something's come up at work, so I'm afraid we'll have to postpone our fishing.'

Unreasonably Rosanne was angry, although she knew they had not even had a firm arrangement. She spoke sharply. 'That's quite all right, Brendan, don't give it a thought, you just go on with what you're doing there.' She waited for further explanation but Brendan had caught her tone and matched it.

'I will,' he said shortly. 'I've said I'm sorry.' He half covered the mouthpiece to mask his voice but Rosanne caught the muffled words 'All right, Mary, I'll be there now.' Then he spoke clearly to Rosanne.

'I'll be back tomorrow, perhaps we can go then.'

'If I'm still here,' said Rosanne and, bitter that he was with Mary, added, 'I'm going to Greece.' There was a moment's silence at the other end and then Brendan said, 'I hope you enjoy yourself. Goodbye,' and rang off.

Slowly Rosanne replaced the receiver and wished she could switch the clock back ten minutes. Why had she spoken to Brendan like that? She had no reason to be angry with him, in fact she had not been looking forward to telling him she was going, and she realized that she had used her anger to smother the feeling of guilt she had about walking out on Ruth and the children.

'Going to Greece?' Ruth had been unashamedly listening to Rosanne's end of the conversation. So Rosanne told her all about it, and Ruth, who could see the excitement in her friend's eyes, said, 'Of course you must go if that's what you want.'

'I do, of course I do,' said Rosanne fervently, 'it's just . . . well, I don't know, I'm enjoying myself here with you and I don't like leaving you in the lurch.'

'You aren't,' said Ruth. 'Brendan's here most of the time. I shan't be lonely, we'll miss you of course, but if George wants you you must go.'

'George only wants me when it suits him,' said Rosanne a little bitterly, 'but I'm used to that.'

'You're used to it and if you're prepared to put up with it, that's up to you. Make the most of the time he does want you.' Ruth spoke without particular emphasis, but she met Rosanne's eyes directly for a moment, disconcerting her, and Ruth's words nagged Rosanne throughout a sleepless night. If she were honest she knew Ruth was right and as she had already taken a step away from George by coming to Ireland and sticking to her decision not to write to him, perhaps this was her chance to break free from a relationship which she knew, deep inside, had no future.

In the morning after making several lengthy telephone calls, Rosanne had all the flight information she needed and at last sent the telegram giving her arrival time in Athens the day after tomorrow, Friday 15th. She had to leave for Dublin the next day. Even with the decision made and the steps to implement it taken, Rosanne felt strangely flat and depressed. The children were all disappointed she was going and Ruth's cheerful chatter about hot sun, blue sea and olive groves made Rosanne more miserable, not less. The thrill she had felt when she opened

George's letter had faded and even the delicious anticipation she always knew before seeing George was missing.

Brendan arrived back after lunch and found Rosanne in the cottage alone about to start packing.

'I thought you were going to Greece,' he said. His dark eyes rested on her face for a moment, not boring into her as she had imagined, but faintly questioning. 'Why?'

She stared at him. 'Why?' she repeated.

'Why are you going to Greece?'

'Because I want to. George has asked me to join him for a week or two.'

Brendan did not pretend he didn't know who George was, he merely said, 'Have a nice time,' and went to find Ruth. Rosanne felt suddenly cold as he left the cottage. The colour drained from her face and catching sight of herself in the mirror she saw her face, pale and pinched, reflected there. Her eyes seemed too big and there were dark smudges below them. She stared at herself and then said aloud to the empty cottage, 'What on earth am I doing?' Her words hung in the air and she repeated them in a whisper. Then deliberately she turned to the telephone and dialled for telegrams.

The moment the cancelling telegram was sent Rosanne felt her heart lift and an exuberant relief as if an enormous weight had been removed from her shoulders. She found herself laughing aloud and then ran out of the house into the sunshine down to the beach to join the others. Ruth was at the water's edge, jumping in the waves with Julie, who screamed with glee as the foam bubbled round her chubby knees, Michael and Clare were digging a huge hole to catch the incoming tide and Brendan was sitting, apparently watching them but with his mind far away. Rosanne sat down beside him and he glanced round, surprised. Neither of them spoke for a moment and then Rosanne said hesitantly, 'Brendan, will you take me fishing this evening?' He showed no surprise at her question, but answered simply, 'If you want to go.'

Ruth came back to join them. 'All packed up?' she enquired. Rosanne shook her head. 'Do you mind if I change my mind?' she asked. Ruth beamed. 'We'd be delighted if you did,' she said. 'It would make our day.' Brendan said nothing.

The air was still that evening and the sea sighed gently against the shore, as Rosanne and Brendan pushed the small boat out from the beach armed with rods and life-jackets. 'Never go out to sea without a life-jacket.' Brendan warned her. 'If you're alone you must wear it, however calm the weather seems. It can change very quickly here. Now there are two of us you needn't put one on, but we always take them with us.'

Brendan rigged the outboard and before long they were putting out across the bay towards the headland where Rosanne and the children had been trapped.

Floating in the more sheltered water Rosanne saw wooden slatted boxes almost submerged in the swelling water. They were about thirty yards apart and tied together with heavy duty rope.

'What are those?' she asked as they passed close by one bobbing lazily in the wake of the boat. 'They keep lobsters in them so that they're alive and fresh when they're needed,' said Brendan. 'You sometimes see the fishing-boats moving from one to another. There are several boats go out from here.' Rosanne had seen these boats coming back into the bay and tying up alongside the little dock to empty their catch into a waiting lorrry, and had thought how small they seemed to brave the open sea far beyond the sheltering headland.

Once they were well clear of the headland Brendan left the outboard ticking over and set up a rod for each of them. Each had a mackerel spinner on the end, a long silver lure which flashed like a darting fish as it was drawn

111

through the water, but armed with an ugly three-pronged barb to hook the hungry mackerel which might pounce greedily.

'Now,' said Brendan, 'I'll show you how to cast.' He handed Rosanne one of the rods. 'Here, look at the reel, when you wind in the line, you close it like this, and when you want it to run free you open it like this.' Rosanne watched carefully and, copying what he did, managed to swing the spinner through tht air to land some yards away into the water. After several practice casts Brendan nodded. 'Not too bad. Just keep up your end of the boat and make sure you don't catch the hook in yourself, or me for that matter. They're very difficult to get out.'

They sat for an hour or more in the gently rocking boat, casting their lines and then gradually winding them in again. Rosanne soon got the hang of casting, the weight of the spinner carrying the line out well away from the boat. Neither of them spoke, the silence was warm and comfortable and yet no silence at all, with the sound of the water bubbling under the boat in a continual mutter, and the waves breaking over the shoreline rocks; gulls cried in the sky above them circling hopefully before acknowledging the dusk and wheeling away to their cliff ledges; others stood singly on prominent rocks, unmoving sentinels; and all the time the hiss of the line snaking out across the water and the whirr of the reel as it wound back in. Rosanne felt completely at peace and knew that at that precise moment there was nowhere in the world she would rather be.

Suddenly the peace was shattered as Brendan shouted, 'I've got one,' and his line shrieked away as the hooked fish tried to pull free. Rosanne watched fascinated as Brendan reeled in furiously and she saw the flash of silver as the fish broke above the water, twisting and turning in its efforts to escape. But gradually, inexorably, Brendan won the battle and with a final jerk flicked the fish into the boat, where it flopped helplessly on the bottom. Quickly he unhooked the barb and then with one of the wooden slats he tapped it sharply on the head and with a last gasping flop, it was still. Brendan looked up at Rosanne and grinned, 'Quite a good size,' he said, 'you can have it for breakfast.'

Rosanne shuddered. 'No, thanks,' she said, 'I don't think I could face it.' Brendan laughed and returned to his rod.

After that Rosanne found herself hoping that if there were any more fish it would be Brendan who caught them, but, in the event, there was none. As the dusk gradually deepened, Brendan reeled in his line for the last time and showed Rosanne how to leave hers safely hooked to itself, before he asked, 'Do you know how to run an outboard?' Rosanne said she did not.

'Then I'll show you, come up here and have a look.' So Rosanne edged her way to the stern of the boat, carefully avoiding the dead fish lying in the bottom, and Brendan demonstrated how the engine worked.

'Now you try,' he said, moving aside to allow her to reach the controls. As he did so he brushed against her and for a moment Rosanne was so aware of him, his powerful masculinity, the strength of his body, that she found herself trembling and her hand shook as she reached out to start the engine. For a split second she felt he must see her reaction and say something even if only in derision, but he said nothing and as the moment elongated she forced herself to say brightly as she clasped the throttle, 'Check petrol is on first, gear in neutral . . . ' and as she recited the instructions he had given her she heard her voice gain in confidence and she started the outboard first pull. She turned in triumph, crying, 'I did it!' and found him watching her steadily. His face broke into the engaging grin so reminiscent of Ruth which he reserved for such few occasions and he said, 'You did indeed. Well done. Now take us home,' and he sat back and left her to negotiate the falling tide and bring them safely back once more to the strand. As they rounded the headland Brendan pointed, 'Look, that's where you and the children got cut off — see there is quite a wide channel in from the sea between those rocks. It's one of the few places round here where you can take a boat in safely.'

Rosanne gazed where he pointed and shuddered. She could see the water churning through a break in the rocks which was wider than anywhere else and she recognized the lopsided gape of the cave that had given them shelter, but the thought of approaching it from the sea as Brendan had done when he rescued them, made her grow cold and she turned the boat away from the evil rocks until they were safely behind and the way to the beach was wide and clear.

'I'm going to Cork again tomorrow.' Brendan's voice broke across her thoughts and she looked up sharply. Was he going to see Mary yet again? She knew from the last phone call that he had been with her. Perhaps Mary had changed her mind and it was all on between her and Brendan once more.

'Do I mind? No!' Rosanne assured herself. 'Why should I mind?' Ruth said Mary mellowed him and he's certainly been less irritating these last few days.' She looked at him for a moment and though he was little more than a silhouette in the gathering dusk, she saw all she knew and loved in Ruth there in Brendan. She had never realized how alike they were, not only in superficial ways, but in depth of character as well; a certain strength and dependability, then sudden humour and explosive tempers, Brendan perhaps less predictable than Ruth, but the more exciting for that. Despite her cascading thoughts Rosanne was surprised to hear herself answering quite normally and easily, 'Are you?'

'Only for a day or so. Perhaps when I

get back you'd like to try some fly-fishing for trout. There's a lake not far where I often go.' He paused and as Rosanne said nothing, went on, 'unless you're tired of fishing.'

'No, I'd love to come.'

'Good,' said Brendan.

8

Next morning Rosanne slept late. Vaguely aware of Ruth creeping round the room she turned to face to the wall and drifted back into a comfortable sleep from which she awoke more refreshed than she had for several days. She lay in bed, watching the sun playing on the white ceiling and the shadows dancing on the wall, and at last acknowledged the strange feeling of uncertainty which had been growing within her. She felt as if she were on the edge of the unknown and she wondered if she had the courage to turn away from the comfortable safety of her life so far and move towards a new life . . . with Brendan.

'There!' she said aloud. 'Now I've put it into words. With Brendan,' and she felt a pang at the thought because she was fairly certain it would not be

119

with Brendan. True, they were no longer at loggerheads the whole time, they enjoyed each other's company now; at least, she amended, she enjoyed his. But apart from the knowledge that he spent time with Mary when he was in Cork, which Rosanne found painful, there were her own feelings to consider. She was by no means sure of them; she could now admit to herself that Brendan O'Neill was important to her, she found herself lonely when he was not there and oddly disturbed when he was, but she also had to admit to herself that that was how she had felt about George. 'Do I feel more this time? When Brendan's there I feel I do — but is it enough to give up my job which I love and am good at and my country, to live in Ireland?' Then she laughed aloud at her own presumption. Brendan had by no means indicated that he wanted her to do any of these things. When they had come ashore last night they had hardly spoken as they walked home from the beach and he had made no effort to touch her or hold her as he had before, and yet Rosanne had felt close to him; there had been a gentle peace between them. Now Rosanne wondered if Brendan had been aware of it too. What had he been thinking as they came home through the darkness? And some words of her mother's echoed in her mind, 'Don't keep digging your feelings up to see how they are growing. Give them time and a chance to develop roots and perhaps the plant will blossom.' It was advice she had given Rosanne when she fell hopelessly in love with the boy next door at the age of fifteen, but as she recalled the words Rosanne felt they were even more appropriate now than they had been then. 'So,' she resolved, 'I'll leave the seeds in the ground and see if a plant grows,' and for a second she had a clear mental picture of Clare's wild cyclamen, glowing and perfect, then still unable to decide if she hoped anything would grow, she got out of bed and began to dress. It wasn't until she was on her way downstairs that she realized that in all her soul-searching she had given George no more than a passing thought. She smiled. The ache of his absence had gone.

The cottage was empty and still. The kitchen was cleared and tidy except for one place laid at the table. Beside it were two notes, one scrawled on the back of an envelope. 'On beach, see you when you surface — R.' and the other a folded paper with her name written boldly across it. She unfolded it and read,

Dear Rosanne,
I've gone to Cork as arranged but should be back late tomorrow evening if I've managed to sort out things there. Then I should have some news for you. Don't get into mischief!
Love, Brendan.

Rosanne scrumpled the note between her fingers and sank on to a chair, her heart beating very fast. What things sorted out in Cork? What news? It could only be Mary. 'Well, that solves any problems about the future,' she sighed. 'No wild cyclamen this time,' and with a tear trickling down her cheek she made herself a cup of coffee.

That evening, when the children were ready for bed, Rosanne felt the need to be alone, to be able to drop the cheerful mask she had been wearing all day.

'Do you think Brendan would mind if I took the boat out?' she asked Ruth.

Ruth looked doubtful. 'Do you know how to run it?' she asked, 'Will you be safe?' Rosanne laughed. 'Yes, of course,' she said. 'He taught me last night, and I brought her in entirely alone.'

'I dare say,' said Ruth, still unconvinced, 'but he was there to help if you got into difficulties.'

'I know, but I'll be all right, don't worry, I'm not planning to go out to sea. I shan't go past the headland.'

Ruth glanced out of the window. It was a beautiful evening, sunny and clear without a breath of wind to stir the trees; even the dancing ladies hung poised and motionless. 'Well, I don't suppose he'd mind,' she said at last, 'but don't forget your life-jacket.'

Rosanne, who had the inexplicable feeling of a school-girl allowed out on an unexpected treat, gave Ruth a quick hug.

'Thanks,' she said, 'I'll be just fine. Don't worry. I'll be back before dark, after all it's light till nearly eleven.'

Ruth grinned. 'Take a rod, you might even catch some mackerel for breakfast. Brendan's was very good this morning, but we really need two to serve everybody.'

Rosanne laughed. 'I'll see what I can do,' and collecting the rod and spinner she had used the night before, she slipped out into the warmth of the evening and made her way down to the strand. As she passed the track which led up to Inchmore House she glimpsed a man walking down. Afraid it would be Paul Hennessy and unwilling to waste more time, she quickened her step so that she was at once out of sight, hidden by the towering hedgerows.

When Rosanne reached the beach she put the rod and life-jacket into the boat and hauled it down across the sand to the water's edge. It was no easy task and she was puffing and panting by the time the waves were lifting the nose of the little boat. She clambered aboard and pushed herself out on to the water with one of the oars, and then when she was well clear of the sandy bottom Rosanne unlocked the engine and let it down into the water. 'Petrol, ignition . . . ' One by one she checked each thing as Brendan had shown her the night before. Then she pulled, the engine spluttered a little and died. She pulled again and the same thing happened. The little boat bobbed gently on the water, drifting farther from the shore as the tide ebbed beneath it. Rosanne was beginning to think she had been over-confident in her ability to handle the boat and as she tried for the fifth time she cried, 'Start, damn you!' Again the engine spluttered and faltered but this time it caught and held and, thankfully, Rosanne pushed it into gear and headed out to the open water of the bay. Once well away from the shore Rosanne killed the motor and for a while drifted with the tide, the little boat riding the swell, a tiny cork on the vastness of the sea. The strange peace she had experienced before again swept through her and Rosanne, though still disturbed by Brendan's note, was able to stand back from her initial emotional response and consider the situation slightly more philosophically. She was ready to admit some strength of feeling for Brendan O'Neill, her original antipathy having completely vanished, but she was by no means sure of the depth of that feeling, of how much she was prepared to give up or adapt to make it possible for her to commit herself to Brendan. 'But now,' she thought, 'it doesn't matter. In fact as he's gone back to Mary it's much better that I'm not entirely involved, it makes it that much easier to forget him when I get home again.' She smiled sadly to herself and recognized a strange emptiness within her. 'Pull yourself together,' she told herself sternly, 'at least he helped you finally break free of George. You can go back to school without either of them on your mind and get down to some good hard work,' but even that prospect failed to cheer her.

The evening sun slid behind the headland, leaving the clear sky a delicate shade of orange. The sea rose and fell about her, turning to slate in the fading light. The daylight would last a little while yet and Rosanne decided to try her hand with the fishing-rod. She had no idea if she was likely to catch anything in the bay, but she had promised Ruth she would not leave the shelter of the headland so she unhooked the line and tried a cast. The bulk of her life-jacket, which she had dutifully put on as soon as the boat was moving, impeded her cast and so safe in the knowledge of a fine calm evening Rosanne discarded it and allowing the boat to drift on the tide, passed a peaceful hour casting and reeling in, allowing her thoughts to range freely without letting them dwell on anything in particular. The tide was ebbing steadily and the next time Rosanne really took note of her position she realized that she had drifted out towards the open sea.

'I must get back,' she said. 'Last go.' And with one final hiss her line sped out across the water. She began to reel in when suddenly the line pulled tight and the rod bent alarmingly.

'I've caught one,' she cried aloud and tried to reel the line as she had seen Brendan do, but the line held firm against her and after a minute or two she realized she must have hooked something in the water. Using one of the oars as a paddle she took the boat towards the end of the line, pausing occasionally to reel in the slackness. At last she reached the end, and in the gathering gloom saw that the hook was buried firmly into the thick rope which linked the row of wooden slatted boxes she had noticed the evening before. She had not realized how dark it had become and as she struggled to release the barbed hook from the sodden hemp she wished she had a torch to help her, or even scissors to cut the line. Then she remembered the little locker tucked under the seat in the bows of the boat. She peered inside and was relieved to find a heavy rubber torch. Gripping it between her knees so that she had both hands free to release the hook, she hauled the rope up into the boat so that she could see better. As she did so the box attached to it bumped gently against the side of the boat. Curious to see if there were any lobsters inside, Rosanne caught hold of the box and shone the torch between two slats to reveal, not shiny lobsters trapped and helpless in the bottom but long rolls or tubes wrapped in shiny grey cloth.

'What on earth . . . ?' Rosanne forgot the hooked line and leant over the side of the boat to see more clearly. 'Seven,' she counted, squinting between the slats seven rolls all different lengths bobbing gently in the water in the box, and beneath them were other packages all wrapped in the same grey cloth.

'That stuff must be waterproof, but what can be inside!' Rosanne tried to open the box but there seemed to be no lid.

So absorbed was she in what she was doing she paid no heed to the throb of an engine approaching; then suddenly she was aware of it and glanced up in horror to find one of the fishing-boats from the village bearing down on her at speed.

'He thinks I'm stealing his lobsters,' she thought and jumped to her feet, letting the box submerge once more, and began waving her arms frantically at the fast approaching boat. He seemed bent on running her down and she shouted out, 'Hey! Look out! Look out!' but her cries were lost in the roar of the engine, and the fishing-boat did not alter course. Panic burst inside her and Rosanne leapt for the stern of the boat, trying to start the outboard so that she could escape from the fishing-boat's path, but she was still not very familiar with the motor and though she tried to calm her fear, she could not see what she was doing and fumbled with the controls.

Suddenly the strong beam of searchlight pierced the darkness and illuminated Rosanne and her boat. For a second relief flooded through her as Rosanne knew that the fishermen had seen her at last and could avoid the collision. But fear welled up again as she realized that though they now had her craft trapped in their searchlight they were taking no avoiding action at all. They were now only yards away and she could see their bow-wave creaming out in a white V across the water as the boat pounded towards her dinghy, about to hit it broadside. Rosanne jumped. Half diving, half falling, she leapt into the water, struggling to get out of the deadly path of the oncoming fishing-boat. With the spotlight dazzling her she had seen nothing of the men on board, but now as she gasped in the water, her clothes dragging her down, she caught a glimpse of the man in the wheelhouse, a swarthy man with long dark hair and very white teeth, which gleamed through his smiling lips. The fishing-boat ploughed broadside into Brendan's dinghy, splitting into two and tossing the pieces and contents aside as if they were so many hayseeds. The boat then circled and turned back towards the wreckage. With the searchlight swinging round in a slow arc the men on board began to search the water.

'They're looking for me,' thought Rosanne, struggling to keep afloat and remembering with a sudden pang the discarded lifejacket. She was about to wave and cry out when something deep within her warned her to keep quiet. If they had wanted her alive they could have picked her up easily enough, without ramming her boat, so as the probing light swung round, Rosanne took a deep breath and submerged for a few seconds until her lungs bursting she had to surface gasping for air. The light continued to swing round, though the engine had stopped and the fishing-boat was now drifting on the tide.

'Kill that light and listen.' The voice came so clearly over the water that Rosanne was startled and was about to submerge again when the light died away and another voice said 'We're too obvious here. Collect the box and let's get out.'

'What about the girl?'

There was a short laugh and the second voice said, 'Terrible, these boating accidents. She really should have gone home in the daylight.'

'Suppose she gets ashore.' The voice was anxious. 'She'd no life-jacket on. The tides on the ebb and the undertow round the headland will carry her out to sea.'

'Should we check once more with the light?'

'No. Too dangerous. It might cause interest ashore. Get that box and let's get on out to the *Queenie Q*.'

By this time Rosanne was indeed having trouble staying afloat. Her clothes were waterlogged and the heavy sweater she had worn against the cool evening air was weighing her down unbearably. She was aware of activity on the fishingboat carried out by torchlight but was too intent on keeping well away from that boat to pay much attention to what they were doing. Her instincts had been right, and though she was certain she must drown as she felt herself drawn by the sea to its open vastness she still felt her danger from the men on the boat was even more immediate.

At last the engine roared to life again and the fishing-boat swung away and headed for the open sea, its propeller churning the water and again submerging Rosanne in its swell. As she struggled back to the surface, her head crashed against something hard and she cried out, gulping sea water as she did so. Desperately she gasped for breath, flailing her arms in the water to protect her from whatever had hit her. As she came in contact again she suddenly realized it was one of the oars from her boat and with a sob of relief she clung to it, letting it support her as she regained her breath and strength and was swept inexorably towards the black teeth of the headland rocks and the ocean beyond.

For a few moments Rosanne could only cling to the oar, exhausted by fear and gradually becoming numb in the cold water. She had no thoughts of saving herself, yet instinct made her hold fast to the oar as the sea pulled her gently but firmly farther away from the land.

It was quite dark and she could see nothing except a darker blackness against the sky, which she supposed to be the end of the headland. There was neither sight nor sound of the fishing-boat and Rosanne knew now how it felt to be really alone. Her heart cried out for Brendan as she knew him lost for ever. Then she heard it. A terrifying sound. Waves breaking, pounding on the rocks, the jagged teeth razor sharp that guarded the end of the headland.

'I must swim,' Rosanne thought, for the first time making a conscious decision, 'I must swim or I'll be dashed on the rocks.' Clutching her oar firmly with one arm she tried to swim with the other, but the sea was too powerful and her waterlogged clothes dragged her down. She managed to struggle free of her heavy jersey and began to make a little progress, but the sound of the breaking waves drew nearer and nearer and she knew she was in increasing danger.

The moon which had been creeping up the sky, a dull yellow ball, now gained enough height to spread a pale silver light across the water and turn the flying spray to flying diamonds. In the feeble light Rosanne could just make out the dark shapes of the rocks and the darker bulk of the cliffs behind; and it was then she realized she might still save herself if she could only stay clear of the rocks for long enough; for she remembered the cave where she had sheltered before. It was here somewhere. Frantically she scanned the shore, trying to pierce the darkness to give her some idea of where the entrance to the tiny inlet and the cave might be. But it was hard to pick out landmarks in the darkness and she was fighting a losing battle to stay clear of the wicked rocks. The oar, so long her life-preserver now led her into danger as it responded to the power of the sea and dragged her with it towards the waiting rocky shore.

Rosanne then made her second conscious decision. She must let go of the oar and try to swim, alone, to safety. Even so she prayed as she let it go 'God give me the strength' and pushing it away she turned away from the shore and swam clear of the outcrop, which received and splintered the oar seconds later. Rosanne felt so cold and tired now that she could hardly move in the water. Everywhere round her the sea swirled and broke into millions of white bubbles, roaring in her ears in a frightening crescendo. Suddenly she saw a patch of calmer water, swelling gently between two fingers of rock and she made her last conscious decision.

'That must be the inlet, and if it isn't I don't care any more,' and with the last ounce of her strength she swam towards the calmer water and with a push from the turning tide found herself beached on the sandy floor of the inlet, unable even to drag herself out of the shallow water sucking and ebbing round her.

9

How long she lay on the sand Rosanne did not know, but the gradually rising tide finally roused her once more to awareness of her continued danger. She crawled up the beach towards the cave and when she was well clear of the water for a while she took stock of the situation. She could either set out across the rocks and try to reach the strand before she was cut off by the tide yet again, or she could wait in the comparative safety of the cave until the tide fell and there was daylight to help her across the rocks.

'If I stay here,' she said, speaking aloud to reassure herself with the sound of her own voice, 'it'll be a long wait and freezing cold. And I'm freezing cold already. But if I try now I may lose my way in the dark and fall in again or get trapped by the water. I must get warmer,' and she stood up and swung her arms heftily like a tram-driver, trying to generate some warmth inside her body. She stamped her feet, squelching in her canvas shoes, and tried as she did so to decide what to do.

'Poor Ruth must be frantic,' she thought. 'Thank goodness Brendan's not at home!' and her heart ached at the thought of Brendan and she dreaded telling him his boat was gone. Ruth. She must get back to set Ruth's mind at rest, and yet her heart failed at the thought of negotiating the long scramble over the rocks in the uncertain moonlight.

'I'll stay here,' she decided. 'It would be just too much if I didn't make it to safety now.' and the spray from a large wave confirmed her decision. She slipped into the dark mouth of the cave. No light penetrated here at all and Rosanne paused, trying to accustom herself to the total blackness. She could see nothing. With hands outstretched before her, she felt her way to the ledge and, feeling for footholds, scrambled up on to it and stretched out to wait for the tide. She was afraid to go to sleep in case she rolled into the water and yet even this fear could not prevent her from closing her eyes. The booming of the water in the cave and the beating of her heart and the imagined roar of the fishing-boat's engine combined into a jumbled nightmare which engulfed her as she dozed fitfully on the narrow ledge. And when she finally awoke it seemed no better, her head was spinning and the noise of the sea was still there, the darkness and the cold were still there, and she was alone. She found herself having imaginary conversations with Brendan and once heard herself confessing that she loved him and he, magically, returned her love and folded her into his strong arms, his safe strong arms and promised she need never be afraid again. And she cried out to him, 'Brendan Brendan! My love!' and then the strength of his arms faded and she was once more alone, cold and shivering on the ledge in the cave.

Rosanne forced herself to think rationally, and realized the water had retreated again, leaving the damp floor of the cave smoothly gleaming in the pale morning. So she slithered down from her refuge and crawled out of the cave onto the tiny beach, blinking and screwing up her eyes against the light. Colour was creeping back to the world; the greys and blacks of dawn gradually gave way to blue sea, green grass on the clifftop and nodding pink thrift in the crevices above. Though the tide had cleared the cave the water was still high and so Rosanne waited a little until she was sure she could gain the strand without difficulty. She knew she ought to get warm again, but the cold had crept deep and she shivered uncontrollably; this time there was no Brendan to rescue her.

At last she set out across the rocks towards the beach; clambering and sliding, grazing her hands as she clutched at sharp edges and always searching the horizon for the approach of the fishing-boat, terrified that they might return and finish what they had started in the night. Killing her. Why? It was only now that the question occurred to Rosanne, but she lacked the energy to consider it and stored it away in the back of her benumbed brain until she could give it more attention. Now her mind concentrated on one thing, and that was reaching the cottage and safety; if possible without attracting attention to herself.

At last she reached the beach, where the sand left smooth by the receding tide sparkled in the early sun. A little warmth had crept back into the air and it made Rosanne shiver even more violently, with her damp clothes clinging clammily to her. Slowly she set off up the hill through the lanes to the cottage, hoping she would meet no one on the way to question why she was so wet and bedraggled. She was lucky, nobody was about so early and the first person who saw her was Ruth.

'Rosy!' she shrieked, rushing to the gate to help her. 'Where the hell have you been? I've been worried stiff. I've got the lifeboat out looking for you.' She hustled the exhausted Rosanne into the cottage and grabbing a blanket from the sofa where it was obvious she had spent the night Ruth wrapped it round her friend and pushed her firmly into a chair.

'Get those wet clothes off,' she ordered, 'and then wrap yourself up in that. Here's a towel,' and she tossed the kitchen towel across to her. 'I'll put the kettle on for a hot drink and I must ring the lifeboat station and say that you're safe.'

Rosanne stripped her wet clothes off, and rubbed herself with the towel, then still shivering she wrapped herself up in the blanket and curled up in the big armchair. Ruth brought her a steaming mug of coffee liberally laced with brandy and then poked the embers which still glowed in the grate, coaxing them to lick round some dry kindling which she put on top. Once certain that the fire was going again she went into the hall to telephone. Rosanne heard her speaking to the lifeboat station.

'Yes, she's safe . . . No. I don't know what has happened I haven't had a chance to talk to her yet; she's obviously been in some trouble because she's soaking wet and very cold. Will you? Fine, we'll be here. Thank you.' The phone dinged and Ruth came back into the living-room. She added more fuel to the fire and then stood staring down at the still shivering Rosanne.

'Well,' she said abruptly.

Rosanne looked at her wearily.

'I'm sorry, Ruth,' she whispered. 'I've lost Brendan's boat.'

'What!'

'A fishing-boat ran me down.'

Ruth stared at her. 'A fishing-boat?'

'Yes, as I was coming in. Well, about to, anyway.'

'But where have you been since then?'

'They left me in the water. The boat

was wrecked and they left me in the water.' Now at last the tears came and Rosanne sobbed, clutching her blanket round her and shuddering. Ruth knelt beside her and held her, there was nothing else she could do until Rosanne's sobs subsided a little. Then she said, 'But didn't they see you? Why didn't they pick you up?'

'Oh yes,' said Rosanne shakily; 'they saw me alright. They ran me down deliberately.'

'Deliberately!' Ruth was incredulous. Rosanne was shivering so hard that she could hardly hold her coffee mug, and Ruth decided to leave further explanations until Rosanne was safely in bed.

'Stay there for a moment,' she said 'I'm going to put a hot-water bottle in your bed and then that's where you're going.'

Half an hour later after a hot bath Rosanne lay thankfully in her bed and with a bottle at her feet and another hugged to her she began, at last, to feel some warmth steal back into her body.

She smiled weakly at Ruth who sat on her own bed and watched anxiously.

'Now, tell me exactly what happened.'

So Rosanne did as best she could, and Ruth listened amazed at the story she told. 'Thank God you're safe,' she said as Rosanne lapsed into silence. 'But you must tell the police when they come and the coastguard.'

'Are they coming?'

'They are. They must hear why the lifeboat was called out.'

'What shall I tell them?'

'What you told me. Did you get a look at the fishermen?'

'The light was in my eyes, but I saw the one in the wheelhouse when I was in the water. I think I'd know him again.'

'And you're certain they ran you down on purpose?'

'Positive. They had plenty of time to steer clear.'

'It must have been because you were looking into the lobster box. Tell me again what you saw.'

Rosanne described again the rolls and packages wrapped in oilskin cloth.

'They must be smuggling in, or out.' Ruth said.

'I suppose so.' Rosanne was not interested, she was wondering now how to tell Brendan about his boat, and she said 'What's Brendan going to say?' Ruth pulled a face. 'I don't know,' she admitted.

'I'd like to tell him myself,' said Rosanne. 'So when he gets here tonight let me speak to him alone.'

'I will,' said Ruth. 'And in the meantime you must get some sleep. If and when the coastguard come to find out what happened I'll wake you, for this all ought to be reported to somebody.'

Rosanne snuggled deeper under the blankets and found her eyes closing in the comforting warmth as the events of the night caught up with her and she slept.

Ruth woke her some time later to say

that the coastguard was downstairs and could she bring him up.

'I'd rather come down,' said Rosanne, 'I won't take a minute to dress.' And so Ruth went down to make coffee while Rosanne pulled on sweater and jeans and dragged a comb through her tangled hair.

The coastguard was waiting in the living-room, drinking a mug of coffee and talking to Ruth. He broke off when Rosanne came into the room and Ruth said, 'This is Rosanne Charlton, Rosy this is Mr Halliday from the lifeboat station.' Mr Halliday, who had risen to his feet, waited until Rosanne was seated with her own coffee and then said, coming straight to the point, 'Now, Miss Charlton, I'm sorry to hear of your accident, perhaps you'd be so good as to tell exactly what happened.' So Rosanne explained and he listened to her without interruption, his steady blue eyes never leaving her face. When she had finished there was silence until he said quietly, 'I suppose you know what you're saying, Miss Charlton, it's a very serious accusation.'

'I know,' said Rosanne in a low voice, 'but it all happened exactly as I described.' The coastguard nodded. 'Then it's a matter for the Garda,' he said. 'They'll come and see you. I should stay at home until they've been.'

Ruth looked alarmed. 'You don't think Rosy's in any danger, do you?' Mr Halliday smiled, 'No, I don't think so, but it would be wise to stay at home until the police have the whole story.'

When he had gone Rosanne said, 'Do you think I'm in any danger from those men?' Ruth considered for a moment and said, 'I don't know. They must have been afraid because of what you saw, and yet you don't really know what you did see; the significance of the things, I mean, but if they think you've drowned you should be safe and when you've talked to the Garda it'll be too late, anyway.'

Rosanne nodded, 'Then I'd better talk to them as soon as possible.'

'Mr Halliday said he'd see them and make his report, but I think I'll phone as well.' Ruth went into the hall and dialled.

It was Garda Murphy who came in answer to Ruth's call, and Rosanne had to tell her story yet again. At first the policeman seemed sceptical, but as Rosanne described what she had seen in the floating box his attitude changed and he listened with marked attention, and when she had finished he got her to sign a statement.

'Now,' he said, ''t'would be a helpful thing if you could identify the man in the wheelhouse. Do you think if we showed you some photos you'd be able?'

Rosanne nodded. 'I think so, I only saw his profile, but I don't think I'll forget that face in a hurry.'

'That would be grand,' said the Garda getting up. 'We'll be in touch. A man may come from Cork tomorrow or the day after. You'll not be leaving us before then, I trust?' Rosanne shook her head and Ruth said, 'Is Miss Charlton in any danger?'

'I doubt it,' replied Garda Murphy. 'It is unlikely the fishing-boat returned and if it did we shall never know which it was as the entire fleet was out last night. As you saw no name or number . . . '

'I couldn't, the searchlight was in my eyes. I only saw the man in the wheelhouse as the boat drew away, and all the rest was in darkness.' Rosanne spoke defensively, the colour rushing to her pale cheeks, and Ruth immediately said, 'It's all right, Rosy,' and put a protective arm around her shoulders. 'She ought to go back to bed,' Ruth turned to the officer, 'She's still very shocked.'

'Of course,' said Garda Murphy sympathetically, 'we'll call again tomorrow or the next day when you are quite recovered, Miss Charlton.'

'Ruth,' said Rosanne, when the policeman had gone, 'I don't think he believed any of what I said.'

'Don't be so silly,' cried Ruth. 'Why should he not indeed?'

'Well, it does sound far-fetched when I tell it in the cold light of day.'

'But whatever reason would you have to be making it up,' said Ruth, her Irish lilt becoming, as usual, more pronounced as she became indignant.

'None, except perhaps to hide the fact that I had lost the boat by my own carelessness to protect myself from blame.'

'Well, I doubt they think that,' said Ruth reassuringly 'and I certainly don't. Now back to bed,' she ordered, but before she could hustle Rosanne upstairs again the telephone rang. Ruth answered it and said with relief, 'It's Brendan. He wants to talk to you.'

10

Rosanne's heart was thumping as she took the receiver but was strangely comforted to hear Brendan's deep voice over the phone.

'Hello, Rosanne? Look, I thought I'd better let you know I shan't be back this evening as I'd hoped, but I'll definitely be there tomorrow evening. I've got a couple of people to see and I can't get out of it.' He paused but Rosanne said nothing. She stared dumbly at the wall; now she would have to wait another whole day before she could tell him about his boat. The hours ahead seemed to stretch into eternity and all were overshadowed by the confession she would have to make when he got home. She felt utterly miserably and was only brought sharply back to the phone in her hand by Brendan saying testily, 'Rosanne. Rosanne, are you there?'

'Yes,' she whispered 'I'm here.'

'That's all right, then. Why didn't you answer?' There was another pause and in it Rosanne made a decision. She would tell Brendan now, she could not leave it until the next day. Silence fell again as she searched for the words to begin and again Brendan spoke sharply.

'Rosanne!' Rosanne took the plunge.

'Brendan. Yes, I'm here. I'm sorry you're not coming this evening, you see I've got something to tell you.'

'Can't it wait, just till tomorrow?'

'No,' Rosanne spoke firmly, her voice stronger now her resolution was made. 'I must tell you now.' Brendan caught the anxiety in her tone and said gently 'All right, tell me. What is it?'

Rosanne took a deep breath and said 'I'm very sorry, Brendan, but I've wrecked your boat. It's smashed to pieces and the engine is lost and your fishing-rod ... ' her voice broke as Brendan, now anything but gentle, exploded down the line.

'You've what! What the hell were you

doing? The boat and the engine! You damn fool woman, what were you doing in my boat?' Without pause for breath he continued to tell her what he thought of her until Ruth, watching Rosanne wilting visibly, snatched the receiver and said sharply, 'Brendan! Shut up!' and in the amazed silence that followed she said more calmly, 'You don't know the half of it, Rosanne's been in great danger and is lucky to be alive at all.' And then briefly she explained what had happened. When she had finished Brendan said, 'Where are the kids? Do they know what happened?'

'No,' said Ruth. 'They were still asleep when she got in and they've gone to Barley Cove for the day with Mrs Tandy and her two boys. I told them Rosy wasn't feeling well, that's all.'

'Good,' said Brendan. 'Make sure they don't find out, the fewer people who know the better.'

'You mean you think Rosanne's in some sort of danger?'

'I don't know, but I don't like the sound of any of it. You make sure you stay with her until I get there tomorrow evening.'

'All right,' agreed Ruth. 'I will. I won't let her out of my sight.'

'Now put her back on the phone,' demanded Brendan.

'Only if you promise not to shout at her,' said Brendan. firmly. 'She's still very shocked and you bawling at her is the last thing she needs.'

'I promise,' said Brendan, 'I'll be gentle as the morning mist.' Ruth grinned and passed the telephone back to Rosanne.

'Hallo,' her voice was hesitant as if she was braced against further recrimination, but Brendan was as good as his word and, seeing Rosanne relax against the wall, Ruth went into the kitchen and left them to each other.

'Rosanne, I'm sorry. I shouldn't have shouted at you.'

'I'm sorry too, Brendan. It's all my fault — your beautiful boat . . . '

157

'Damn the boat, as long as you're all right.'

'I'm all right.'

'That's my girl. Now listen, you mustn't be alone until I get there, some time tomorrow evening. It sounds to me as if there's more to this than meets the eye. Goodness knows what you've stumbled on to. Are you sure that the fishermen didn't just panic because they sunk you?'

Remembering the face of the man in the wheelhouse of the fishing-boat Rosanne shuddered.

'No, he ran me down deliberately and then left me to drown. Honestly, Brendan, I know it wasn't an accident. You must believe me.' Her voice cracked as she spoke and Brendan said, 'I do believe you. Don't get upset, I just wanted to be sure.'

'I am.'

'Right. Well, there's probably no danger, but I'd be a sight happier if I knew you stayed with Ruth all the time. Darling — are you listening?' Rosanne could hardly believe her ears — surely he had called her 'darling'. Her thoughts were in a turmoil and she paid scant heed to the rest of his advice. 'Don't tell the children or anyone else what has happened, certainly until you've identified the men from the Garda's pictures.' Rosanne did not answer and he said again, 'Rosanne, are you listening?' Rosanne gave herself a mental shake and said, 'Yes, of course.'

'Good. Well, I'll see you tomorrow and in the meantime stay with Ruth and be careful.'

'I will,' promised Rosanne. Brendan's voice softened again. 'See you,' and he rang off. Very slowly Rosanne replaced the receiver, and steadied herself before joining Ruth in the kitchen.

'What did he say?' asked Ruth looking up.

'He said to stay with you and he'd be home tomorrow.'

'Fine. Well, back to bed with you.'

'I'm all right,' Rosanne protested, but Ruth was adamant.

'Go back to bed for now at least. I'll bring you something on a tray, you must be starving. Then if you're really feeling better you can come down again when the kids are in bed and I'll beat you at Scrabble.'

Rosanne laughed for the first time that day. 'Bully!' she said. 'All right.' She turned to the door and then paused, 'Thank you, Ruth.'

'Go on with you,' scolded Ruth, 'bed.'

Later that evening when the children were safely tucked up and asleep Rosanne put on her dressing-gown and slippers and went downstairs to join Ruth. She had slept again and now felt much better, almost her normal self and since her conversation with Brendan she had an insistent flicker of hope inside. He had called her 'darling' even if a little irritably, almost as if he had not noticed it. Rosanne found herself longing to see him again, to be able to search his face for his true feelings, and yet fearing the encounter and the promised news he had to bring. In her head she was sure he was going to break the news about Mary and him meeting again, yet her heart told her not to believe it until he had actually done so. She longed to talk to Ruth about him, but was afraid of betraying herself and her feelings to her ever-perceptive friend, so she hardly mentioned him, except in passing conversation.

As they were finishing supper there was a knock at the back door and Paul Hennessy breezed in without waiting for an invitation.

'Hallo, girls,' he cried cheerfully. 'How's life?' Then he noticed Rosanne's dressing-gown and said slightly abashed, 'I say, I'm sorry, are you going to bed already?'

'No, Rosanne's not been well today,' replied Ruth, 'Coffee?'

'Yes, please,' said Paul. 'Sorry to hear that, Rosy, nothing serious, I hope.'

'No,' said Rosanne 'I'm better now.'

'Rosanne had an accident in Brendan's boat,' explained Ruth as she busied herself making coffee. 'She capsized in the bay last night and has spent the day recovering.'

'From a ducking?' Paul's laugh was faintly derisive and Ruth leapt to Rosy's defence. 'She spent the night out there on the rocks, cut off by the tide so it was slightly more than a mere ducking.' She spoke sharply and Paul looked suitably sorry but before he could speak Rosanne said, 'Never mind, Ruth.' Remembering Brendan's warning she was anxious to change the subject before they went into any more detail.

'Any news of your pictures, Paul?'

'Oh, you heard about those, did you?' Paul's interest appeared diverted. 'No, nothing yet. The police say it's one of several similar robberies in this part of the country.'

'Did you lose anything else?' asked Ruth, handing him his coffee. 'Garda Murphy was here asking questions, whether we'd seen lights or heard a car go up the lane, but he only mentioned the pictures.'

'One or two small items of jewellery my wife had left down here.'

Then he turned the conversation back again. 'How did you come to capsize, Rosy? There was no sea running last night.'

'Collision,' said Rosanne briefly. 'The coastguard knows all about it.'

Paul whistled. 'That must account for it,' he said. 'There was a lot of activity out in the bay this afternoon, a police boat and a coastguard launch. Were they looking for your boat, do you think?'

'I don't know,' said Rosanne wearily. 'But I'm trying not to think about it now, if you don't mind, Paul. It was all like a nightmare and I want to forget it.'

Paul was contrite at once and said, 'Of course you do. I'm sorry I didn't mean to harp on it. Where is Brendan today? Does he know about the boat?'

'He's in Cork,' answered Ruth. 'He'll be back tomorrow evening, I expect. He's still busy doing his research, and every now and then he gets called back to work as a new stage is reached. Are you with us much longer?'

'A few more days, I expect,' replied Paul casually. 'It all depends on a bit of business I have in hand. I may leave even sooner.' The conversation flagged then, neither Ruth nor Rosanne were anxious to prolong it and so when he had finished his coffee Paul Hennessy got up to go. 'Hope you'll be recovered quite soon,' he said to Rosanne. He treated them to his most charming smile, and said goodnight. As he reached the door he turned once more to Rosanne and asked suddenly, 'Who did you collide with?'

Taken a little off guard Rosanne replied, 'A fishing-boat.' Paul raised his eyebrows. 'A fishing-boat! Didn't you see it?'

'Apparently it didn't see me.'

Ruth was irritated by the way Paul kept asking questions and she snapped at him, 'For God's sake, Paul, don't go on so. Rosy's had enough. If you must know they ran her down and then left her to drown. The Garda are bringing some photos for her to look through tomorrow or the next day, then with any luck we'll know who did it. In the meantime give her a break, will you? Leave her alone.'

Taken aback at her outburst Paul apologized again and beat a hasty retreat and Ruth shut and locked the back door behind him.

'Thank goodness he's gone,' she exclaimed as she rejoined Rosanne by the fire. 'I know he didn't mean any harm but really . . . '

Rosanne sighed. 'I wish in a way he didn't know anything about it,' she said. 'We weren't going to tell anyone Ruth.'

'I know,' admitted Ruth wearily, 'perhaps I shouldn't have said anything, but I don't suppose it'll matter. It's only Paul and, anyway, the whole village probably knows if what he said about the Garda and the coastguard is true. You can't keep secrets in a place like this.'

'What do you suppose they were

doing?' asked Rosanne. 'Do you really think they were looking for the boat — well, the bits, I mean?'

'I doubt it,' said Ruth 'I shouldn't think there'd be much to find, would you? I mean, there's been a couple of tides since then. I'd have thought they were probably looking in the other lobster boxes.'

'For more oilskinned parcels, you mean?'

'Yes. But if I were the men on the fishing-boat I'd have made very sure there was nothing for anyone to find by this morning.' It was Ruth who sighed now as she said, 'God, I do wish Brendan was here. He'd know what to do.'

'So do I,' echoed Rosanne in her heart but all she actually said was, 'Well, he'll be here tomorrow evening, then he can sort things out with them all. I must say I'd feel easier, too, with him here.' She smiled ruefully, 'I'm sorry this has all happened, Ruth; I haven't made your holiday any easier at all — quite the opposite in fact.' Ruth laughed, back to her usual cheerful self. 'Well, it's been different, at least we've not had a dull moment. And Brendan being here has made a difference too, he always livens the place up.' She looked at Rosanne with the hint of a twinkle in her eye and added, 'Don't you think, Rosy?' Rosanne kept her face impassive. She was not prepared to discuss Brendan with anyone, especially Ruth; so she merely replied, 'Yes, he seems fun,' and then got up.

'I think I'm going to bed, Ruth, if you don't mind and then tomorrow I'll be ready for anything.' If she had realized what tomorrow would bring she might not have spoken so flippantly, but she did not and, in contrast to the nightmares of the previous night, her sleep was dreamless and deep.

11

Next day was dull and grey with heavy overcast skies, not at all the weather to encourage them on to the beach, so Ruth bundled everyone into the car and drove them to the nearest market town to spend their holiday money. The children clutched the pound-note their father had given each of them to spend and set about that serious business. Rosanne suggested that they split up to speed the operation, but Ruth was adamant.

'I'm not letting you out of my sight, Rosy,' she said. 'Now, then, what about going into O'Shea's and exploring the toy department?' They all went into the shop, clattered upstairs to the display of toys on the first floor, and the choosing began.

At last after more than half an hour they emerged triumphant, Michael with a very noisy cap pistol, Clare with a beach ball and Julie wearing three necklaces. 'Coffee, I think,' said Ruth, exhausted by the business of the morning. 'No, Clare, you can't change your mind again, it's a lovely beach ball,' and she led the way into a little café where the children could eat huge ice-creams, and Rosanne and Ruth could sit and relax over coffee and some beautiful apple cake. By the time they had done the household shopping as well they were ready for lunch and drove back to the cottage.

The telephone was ringing as they walked in through the door and Ruth called to Rosanne to answer it while she unloaded the children and the shopping. A moment later Rosanne rushed into the front garden, where Ruth was struggling with a box of groceries, crying, 'Ruth, hurry, it's David for you.' With a shriek of 'David!' Ruth dumped the box into Rosanne's waiting arms and ran into the house, and Rosanne followed her more slowly carrying the shopping.

The two older children had realized who was on the phone and were jumping up and down shouting, 'It's Daddy! Can I talk to Daddy? I want to talk to Daddy.' Julie, infected by their excitement, twirled round and round with her arms stuck out sideways chanting, 'Dad-dy Dad-dy Dad-dy.' Suddenly Ruth put her hand over the mouthpiece and roared, 'Quiet, the lot of you! I can't hear a word Daddy's saying.' Rosanne hustled the children out of the hall and shut the door so that Ruth could have some peace, though the noise continued in the kitchen.

'I wanted to talk to Daddy,' wailed Clare.

'I was going to tell him about my gun,' said Michael. 'Can I talk to him in a minute?'

'I don't know,' said Rosanne, hugging Clare to try and cheer her up. 'Daddy's a long way away and he may only be able to talk to Mummy this time.'

'It's not fair,' muttered Michael, 'it's

always Mummy's turn.'

Suddenly the door opened and Ruth came into the kitchen, her eyes shining and her cheeks flushed with excitement.

'Darlings, guess what? That was Daddy phoning and he's arriving today.'

'What!' Rosanne exclaimed, but her voice was drowned by the cries of delight and excitement from the children.

'Listen! Listen!' cried Ruth, raising her voice above the hubbub. 'He's in London and he's got a seat on a flight to Cork which arrives at six o'clock this evening. Isn't that grand? He'll be here for the rest of the holiday.' The children cheered wildly and Ruth suddenly hugged Rosanne and said, 'Oh, Rosy, I'm so excited. I do miss him so when he's away.'

'How's he managed to get back so soon?' asked Rosanne returning Ruth's hug.

'Oh, I'm not sure exactly; he said something about trouble out there so they've all been sent home. Anyway, whatever it is, he arrived in London late last night and has been trying to get hold of us all morning.'

'That's marvellous,' said Rosanne 'and you can all go and collect him at the airport.'

'Yes, that's what he thought; so if we get organized here after lunch we can set off in plenty of time to meet the plane.'

'Well,' said Rosanne, 'I won't come. For one thing there won't really be enough room in the car coming back, and for another it's a family occasion, I'd be in the way.'

'Nonsense,' protested Ruth. 'Of course you wouldn't.'

'Well, I'm not coming, anyway. I'll stay here and cook supper so when you all come in starving it'll be ready to dish up.'

Ruth was still worried. 'We shouldn't leave you alone here,' she said. 'Brendan said we were to stay together until he got here.'

'But Brendan didn't know David was going to arrive, did he?' said Rosanne reasonably. 'Anyway, he'll probably be here himself soon after you've gone. It'll still be daylight, nothing's going to happen to me in broad daylight. Let's face it, it won't even be dark by the time you get back. I'll be fine.' And before Ruth could protest any further Rosanne changed the subject. 'Now about beds. I'll move in with the children, that's the best thing then you and David can have our room and with luck a little peace and privacy.'

Ruth laughed, 'What, with our kids around? You're joking! They use our bedroom as a general meeting-place — it gets like Piccadilly Circus some mornings. Are you sure you don't mind moving in with the children for a couple of nights? When Brendan's not here you could have his room, or you might find it more peaceful on a campbed down in the living-room.'

'Don't worry about me,' said Rosanne cheerfully, 'I'll be quite happy in the bottom bunk; at the most it'll only be for ten days,' and she felt a sudden pang as she realized how little time she had left before she had to leave Ireland to return to England, her quiet flat and her new job. Leave Ireland — and Brendan.

Ruth and the children set off at about four o'clock, leaving the cottage clean and tidy and the bedrooms altered as planned. As she climbed into the car Ruth looked anxiously at Rosanne.

'You will be careful Rosy, won't you? Stay in the house and lock the door. You won't go out on your own, will you? Promise?' She was so insistent that Rosanne said, laughing, 'Yes, yes, I promise, I won't go out alone.'

'And lock the door,' repeated Ruth. 'Don't open it to anyone except Brendan or the Garda.'

'Don't worry,' soothed Rosanne, 'I won't. Now off you go or David'll have landed and you won't have been there to meet him.'

Ruth started the engine and with a

final wave backed the car out into the lane and disappeared into the dull grey afternoon.

It was strangely silent when they had gone and Rosanne was suddenly aware of being alone with only the continuous burbling stream for company, and with a slight shiver she went indoors. Remembering her promise to Ruth she solemnly locked the door behind her, then she went to the back door and locked that too.

'Of course if anyone really wanted to get in, a couple of locked doors are hardly going to stand in their way.' Rosanne spoke aloud and was a little reassured by the sound of her own voice, though not by her thoughts themselves; but with her usual common sense she put such thoughts behind her and armed with one of the library books on Irish history she had brought with her, she settled herself down to wait for Brendan or Ruth, whoever should arrive first.

At about six she stirred herself and

reluctantly leaving her comfortable chair and fascinating book, set about preparing a casserole for supper. It was the obvious meal to cook, for she could make it large enough to feed everyone if necessary and it could sit happily in the oven until they were ready to eat.

She had just finished and popped the dish into the oven when the silence round her was shattered by the shrill of the telephone. Her heart was beating as she lifted the receiver, certain it was Brendan calling to say he could not come, but to her surprise it was Ruth's voice she heard.

'Hallo, Rosy, is that you? Can you hear me? It's a terrible line.' It was indeed and Rosanne had difficulty in hearing what Ruth was saying above the crackle and hiss on the line.

'Yes, it's me,' Rosanne almost shouted. 'Can you hear me?'

'Barely,' came the reply. 'Listen, Rosy, bad news. Cork airport is fogged in. David's plane can't land. They've made two attempts, but each time they've changed their mind so now he's been diverted to Shannon.'

'Where?' said Rosanne, missing the destination.

'Shannon,' repeated Ruth. 'Then they'll be brought here by bus.'

'However long will that take?' asked Rosanne.

'A good three hours, the man says, may be more.'

'What'll you do?'

'Well, by the time I've driven back down to you it'll be time to turn round again, so I think we'll wait.'

'Can you manage with the children?' Rosanne could think of nothing worse than having three young children hanging round an airport for three hours.

'Well,' cried Ruth, above the continued crackling, 'there's nothing to do here, so I'll take them into Cork city to the pictures or something. There's a Walt Disney programme at one place, I see from a poster.'

'Good idea,' said Rosanne. 'Don't

worry I'll turn the supper down and we'll expect you when we see you.'

'Is Brendan there yet?' asked Ruth anxiously.

'No, not yet, but I'm fine,' Rosanne reassured her. 'He'll be here soon. It's only half past six or so.'

'Well, don't go out by yourself,' reminded Ruth.

'I won't. See you later.'

'See you.' And Ruth rang off.

Rosanne turned the oven down very low and then decided a drink might cheer her up and pass the time till Brendan put in an appearance. She poured herself a gin-and-tonic and carried it to her seat by the fire. The evening was a miserable grey outside and Rosanne poked the logs until they blazed cheerfully. 'It's more like January than August,' she remarked and reached once again for her book.

She had only read a page or so when there was a sharp knock on the front door. Startled she jumped up, her book falling to the floor. It was no good pretending not to be at home, which was her first reaction; whoever it was could see her easily through the living-room windows.

Anyway, perhaps Brendan had forgotten his key, or maybe it was the Garda with the photographs for her to study; yet she had not heard a car of that she was certain.

Warily she went to the front door and called out, 'Who is it?' and a wave of relief flooded through her as she heard Paul Hennessy's voice saying 'It's me, Paul. Can I come in?'

'Of course,' said Rosanne and unlocked the door. He beamed at her.

'Are you on your own or babysitting? I see there's no car outside.' He followed her into the lamplit sitting-room, his gaze quickly taking in the gin and the book.

'On my own for a while,' said Rosanne more cheerfully than she felt. To tell the truth, she had begun to find her own company in the quiet cottage a little irksome and was glad to see Paul

Hennessy, though she had a feeling that the time was coming when she might have to fend him off if they were close together for too long. Then she explained about Ruth and the children rushing off to Cork to meet David.

'How exciting for them,' said Paul, 'but you've been left alone to drink in solitary state until they get back.'

'Oh,' said Rosanne 'I'm sorry, would you like a drink?'

'What a nice thought,' said Paul. 'But here's a better one. Instead of sitting here waiting for the wanderers' return. why don't we walk up to Inchmore and have a drink there? I can show you the house and some of my treasures.'

'But I thought . . . ' began Rosanne, and then stopped selfconsciously.

'That they'd all been stolen?' Paul finished for her. 'No, I've many beautiful things left, even though the thieves took some of the most valuable and the things most readily converted into cash.' He took her hand and squeezed it gently, 'Will you not come up and have a drink with me. You'll be back well before Ruth, I have an appointment myself later.' Retaining his grasp on her hand he led her towards the door and Rosanne, tired of her own company, smiled and said 'All right, I'd like that, but only for a little while, I've a casserole in the oven. Give me a minute to make myself tidy,' and she slipped upstairs to powder her nose and freshen her neck and hair with a generous spray of perfume from the atomiser on her dressing-table. She regretted this last action as when she joined Paul in the living-room he sniffed appreciatively and said, 'Mm, you smell delicious.' His eyes lingered on her for a moment and to cover her embarrassment she said brightly, 'Let's go then, I mustn't be long. 'Oh, perhaps I should leave a note for Brendan, just to say where I am.'

Paul raised his eyebrows a little and said pointedly, 'Like that is it? He has to know your movements?'

Rosanne felt the colour flood to her

cheeks. 'No, of course not. It's just that he thinks I'll be here.'

'So you will,' said Paul soothingly, 'we'll just have a quick drink, unless you'd rather not come at all?'

Rosanne suddenly felt she would rather not go but she felt it would be very rude to back out now, so she forced a smile and said, 'Don't be silly, Paul, I'd love to come.'

'Good,' said Paul and opened the front door. As she closed it behind them Rosanne heard the faintest echo of Ruth's warning, 'Don't go out alone,' and thought happily, 'I'm not breaking my promise because Paul is with me and I'm sure he'll see me home again.' As they started up the track to Inchmore House Paul took Rosanne's arm to guide her over its unevenness.

'Did the Garda come with the photographs yet?' he asked casually.

'No, not yet,' replied Rosanne. 'I'm not even sure they believed what I told them. They don't seem to have taken it seriously.'

'But you wouldn't have made it up,' exclaimed Paul, and Rosanne felt his grip on her arm tighten.

'No, but they probably think it was an accident and the fisherman lost his nerve and decided not to report it.'

'That's a possibility, I suppose,' agreed Paul. 'Now then, here we are, Inchmore House,' and they paused at the gate to admire it as it stood four-square, its windows in symmetrical rows and topped with a grey slate roof and two huge chimneys. Rosanne turned and looked behind her and saw that the house had an unrivalled view out across the cliffs to the sea beyond edged with rocks and boiling foam. Brendan's cottage, nestling among the fucshia bushes at the bottom of the lane, was hardly visible.

'What a glorious view,' she breathed and Paul said, 'Exceptional, isn't it?' and turning from it led the way into his house.

12

Rosanne followed him slowly into the house, and found it strange and rather sombre inside, cold with disuse. The front door gave into a large hall, several panelled doors opened off it and a wide staircase curved upwards to the landing above. Most of the furniture was old and heavy; there was a solid hall table draped with a dull red chenille cloth with two beautifully carved oak chairs set on either side of it. An old oak dresser stood against the wall, displaying matching china dishes, and some little figurines, and a huge grandfather clock ticked solemnly in the corner. The hall was lit by only one square window and it was gloomy when Paul shut the front door. He switched on the lights and the place was immediately more cheerful.

'Here we are,' he said genially. 'You

see they didn't take any of my china,' he waved a hand vaguely at the dresser. 'Probably thought it would break and be worthless. Lucky they didn't just smash it for the hell of it, really. That often happens these days. Come on through, we'll go into the library, there should be a fire in there.' He led the way across the hall and opening one of the doors ushered Rosanne into the room beyond. It was clearly the room where Paul spent most of his time, combining office, library and sitting-room. Some logs smouldered in the grate and as Paul poked them into life again, Rosanne took in the room. Two tall windows looked out on to the garden and beyond to the sea, and set between these was a wide leather-topped desk with a telephone on it and a leather-backed chair. Two walls were lined with books and gapingly empty on the other walls were several picture frames with the pictures neatly removed.

'Now then,' said Paul, when he had

coaxed a flame in the fireplace, 'a drink. Do sit down,' he indicated one of the deep leather armchairs beside the fire and turned to a drinks trolley in the corner.

'What'll it be? Gin, Scotch, Irish?'

'Gin, please,' said Rosanne, 'with a lot of tonic, if you have it,' and she sank comfortably into the chair by the fire. 'I'm glad I came,' she thought as she stretched out her hands to the warmth, 'but perhaps I should have left that note in case Brendan or Ruth get there and worry about me, I really mustn't stay too long.' She said as much to Paul, who replied, 'Don't worry, we'll keep an eye out of the window and if a light comes on down in the cottage we can phone at once and say you're here.'

'That's fine, then,' said Rosanne and relaxed into the chair. Paul handed her her drink, but instead of taking the other armchair he perched on the arm of hers, his arm resting along its back just behind her head.

'Well, this is nice and cosy,' he said

smoothly. Rosanne felt uncomfortable with him sitting up above her, for it meant she had to turn sideways and look up at him. She shifted her position uneasily and took a sip of her drink.

'Oh!' she gasped 'it's a bit strong, Paul, do you think I could have a little more tonic?'

'Of course,' said Paul and took her glass. While he was at the drinks trolley Rosanne stood up and made pretence of looking at the books which lined the walls.

'What lovely books!' she said as if to explain her escape from the chair.

'Yes, indeed,' said Paul handing her the more dilute drink and resuming his place on the arm of the chair. Rosanne calmly sat in the other and Paul said, 'Not feeling antisocial, are you? Why sit way over there?' Rosanne did not answer, but said brightly, 'Do you look after yourself when your wife doesn't come down with you?' She laid faint emphasis on the word 'wife' but Paul appeared not to notice and smiled easily, 'Well there's a man locally who keeps an eye on the place when I'm not here and gives a hand around when I am, chopping logs — general handyman. Sean Malley. He'll be in with some more logs, I expect,' he added, eyeing the depleted log-box by the grate.

'But you do your own cooking?' went on Rosanne, anxious to keep the conversation going at a very mundane level.

'Yes, I'm quite a good cook,' laughed Paul. 'Let me cook you dinner this evening and we'll make a night of it.'

'Well, that's very kind,' began Rosanne hesitantly, longing now to escape back to the safe loneliness of the cottage, 'but I'm cooking for the others so I'll have to go back soon.'

'Your casserole is safely in the oven,' said Paul, moving across and leaning over her chair. 'Stay with me a while, lovely Rosy, stay with me a while and make friends.'

He placed a hand on Rosanne's

shoulders so that she was unable to get up and slipping his other arm round her to cup her breast with his hand, began kissing her hair, her neck and her face. She struggled to get free pushing him away, saying, 'Paul, please don't do that, Paul!'

He released her and said chidingly, 'Oh come on, Rosy. We're both adults. You're a very attractive woman. There's no harm ... ' But Rosanne cut him short. 'I'd like to go home now, Paul.' Paul was immediately soothing. 'Calm down, Rosy, you haven't seen all my treasures yet. Do stay for a little longer, I promise I won't lay a finger on you!'

'Etchings!' thought Rosanne and with some misgiving said, 'All right, I'll finish my drink before I go.' 'Good,' purred Paul, 'that's better. Let me top it up for you.' And he whisked her glass away before she could protest. As she waited for the glass to be returned to her Rosanne remembered Ruth's comment, 'From what Brendan says, all women are his type,' and in different circumstances she would have laughed at its aptness. When he had handed Rosanne her drink Paul sat, very sedately, in the chair opposite her and smiled easily, his bright blue eyes shining with laughter, so that Rosanne found herself smiling back.

'Now, is that better?' he said. 'Tell me, have you quite recovered from your accident?' Before Rosanne could answer either question, the door opened and a dark-haired man came in carrying an armful of logs to replenish the log-box.

'Ah, Malley,' said Paul. 'I should think that'll see me through this evening.' Malley smiled and tumbling the logs into the box said, 'Right you are, sir, I'll be off then,' and turning he quietly left the room.

'Now we've plenty of wood' remarked Paul. He was about to toss another log into the hearth when he caught sight of Rosanne. She was deathly pale and her face was a frozen mask of fear.

'My dear girl,' he cried, all concern,

'what on earth is the matter?'

'That man,' she whispered. 'That man.'

'Malley? What about him. I said he was my odd-job man.'

'He's the man on the boat.'

'The man on the boat?' Paul sounded puzzled. 'What boat?'

'The boat. The fishing-boat. The one that ran me down. He was the man in the wheelhouse.' Rosanne almost screamed at him in her efforts to make him understand. 'Paul, he's the man that tried to kill me. We must call the police.'

Paul looked across at her and said carefully. 'Now, you are quite sure, Rosanne, aren't you? I mean it was dark and you were frightened and in the water. It's quite an accusation unless you are absolutely certain.'

Rosanne returned his steady look and said quietly, 'I'm absolutely certain. I could never, never forget that smile.'

Paul nodded. 'Right!' he said and then raising his voice called out

'Malley!' Immediately the door opened and the man came in.

'You called, sir?' He appeared so quickly that Rosanne suddenly realized he must have been standing right outside the library door. Waiting. She spun round to Paul, who said, 'I'm afraid Miss Charlton has recognized you, Malley. She has no doubt that you're the man in the fishing-boat.'

'Now, that's a great pity, sir,' said Malley. 'What'll we do about that, sir?'

Rosanne's eyes widened in horror as she realized the import of what Malley had said. She stared at Paul. His blue eyes, recently so warm with laughter, now glittered, cold and dangerous.

'It is a difficult situation. I'm inclined to think we have little choice in the present circumstances.'

Rosanne had been very afraid, but now her fears gave way to anger and her pale cheeks flushed.

'You!' she spluttered with rage. 'You're behind all this. You knew who had tried to kill me.' She leapt to her feet but was pushed roughly back into her chair by Malley.

'It was unfortunate that you became involved, and having learned the dangers of that involvement continued to cause trouble. We had to know exactly how much trouble you could cause. I couldn't have Sean in hiding any longer. I need him.'

'So you asked me here to see if I would recognize him.'

'Exactly, my dear. And you did recognize him and, what is more said so, instead of keeping your mouth sensibly shut.'

'Because I thought you were a friend!'

'Precisely, and a dear friend I would have loved to have been in altered circumstances.' Paul strolled across to his desk and slid open a drawer. From it took an ugly snub-nosed gun and placed it gently on the desk top before he continued, 'In fact I have already stood friend to you. Sean was all for silencing you permanently at once, where as I suggested that we test you first. After all, as I said earlier, you're a very attractive woman, Rosy, I didn't want to see you hurt unnecessarily.'

Rosanne dragged her gaze away from the gun on the desktop still within easy reach of Paul's hand and looked round her for a way of escape but there was none. Paul was immediately in front of her, blocking the way to the windows, and Malley was between her and the door. Even if there had been no gun, escape would have been impossible.

'Well?' repeated Malley 'what do we do?'

'An unfortunate accident, I think,' replied Paul smoothly. 'Keep her locked in the attic bedroom until it's dark and then we'll transfer her to the *Queenie Q*. Rosanne recognized the name she'd heard while struggling in the water, though she had quite forgotten it till now.

'And then,' continued Paul, 'she'll merely have disappeared. Her body will probably never be found. If it is it'll be presumed an accident. You might tow one of the dinghies out from the beach and leave it drifting.'

'Right,' said Malley and then shook his head sadly. 'Some people never learn, two boating accidents in a week. Come on, you.' He grabbed hold of Rosanne's arm. Paul smiled his charming meaningless smile at her and said, 'So sorry it had to end like this, my dear. I'd hoped for such a pleasant evening.' His voice hardened and he said, 'but you really have become a great nuisance. Thanks to you a great deal too much interest is being shown in the lobster-pots. Pretty little girls like you should mind their own businesses and keep their mouths shut.'

Rosanne stared at him for a second and then mustering all her strength spat full in his face. For a split second he was amazed as her spittle ran down the side of his nose to the corner of his mouth, then with a sudden movement his hand flashed up and he struck her a resounding blow on the side of her head so that her ears sang and a huge red weal appeared on her cheek.

'Bitch!' He spat the word out and mopped at his face with a handkerchief.

Rosanne expected him to threaten her with the gun, but he appeared to have forgotten it or perhaps he knew there was no need for it, because he only snapped, 'Take her upstairs, Malley.'

Rosanne knew she had very little chance of escaping from a locked room at the top of the big old house and so as Malley forced her towards the stairs, she suddenly bent her head and sank her teeth into his hand. He cried out and for a second released his grip. She twisted free and made a dash for the front door, but someone had drawn the great bolts across and before she could drag them clear Malley was on her again, though she kicked out at him and scratched at his face he soon had whipped one of her arms up behind her back and shouted in her ear, 'One more trick like that and I'll break your bloody arm,' and he jerked it hard, making Rosanne cry out in pain.

'Upstairs!'

Malley shoved Rosanne towards the staircase, past the library door, which was already closed, as if Paul Hennessy had dismissed her from his mind and was concentrating on the next problem. Rosanne stumbled up the stairs as Malley propelled her along in front of him, across the landing and up a second flight, much narrower and more twisting and at length they came to a passage which appeared to run the length of the house. It was floored with bare boards and their footsteps echoed in the emptiness. Still keeping a firm grip on Rosanne's arm Malley opened one of the doors leading from the passage and pushed her into the room beyond.

'You can shout and scream as much as you like up here,' he sneered. 'There's no one to hear you.' He half closed the door and then poked his head in again. 'I'll be back with my friend Brian when it's dark. Don't go away!'

The door slammed and Rosanne heard the key turn in the lock, Malley's footsteps died away along the landing and then there was silence.

13

Rubbing her bruised arm and trying to ease her twisted shoulder, Rosanne stared for a long moment at the closed door, and then aching, angry and frightened, she flopped on to one of the two old iron bedsteads, left over from the days of living-in domestic help, which almost filled the room. Though they were covered with faded quilts, neither had a mattress over the metal mesh of the bed, and groaning, Rosanne crawled off again, deciding she would be more comfortable on the floor. As she lay on the bare boards her head pillowed on her arms, misery and helplessness overwhelmed her and the tears, never far distant during the last two days, began to stream down her face. She cried for herself and she cried because Brendan would never know what had happened to her. If everything went as Paul Hennessy planned, Brendan would believe she had drowned while trying to collect more evidence to convince the Garda of her story; and Paul Hennessy would get away with whatever he was doing, her murder included.

The thought of the hateful Paul Hennessy probably still downstairs like a vile spider weaving plans from the centre of his web, made her anger overcome her misery, and with new resolution she determined to do all she could to ruin those plans.

Immediately she began to think.

'The best thing to do is to try to escape,' she said, speaking aloud to herself as she so often did when confronting a problem. 'Door first.' She went and rattled the handle even though she already knew it was locked. Then she knelt down and peered through the keyhole, but the key had been removed and she had nothing with her with which to try to pick the lock, even if she had had the first idea how to go about it.

The door itself was old and solid and after one attempt to batter it down with her shoulder she gave up.

'I'll never shift that,' she said. 'Now, what next?' And she turned her attention to the window. It was a small casement window tucked up under the roof of the house. It had not been opened for some time and it moved very stiffly, squeaking in protest as it did so, but at last she forced it wide enough to get her head and shoulders through. Standing on the end of the bed she leant out and peered down into the garden below and then wished she had not. She shuddered as she saw the drop to the paved terrace below and drew back hastily; there was no escape that way, the walls of the house were bare and white, impossible to climb up or down.

'Perhaps I can attract someone's attention by waving something,' she thought, 'A bedspread, perhaps,' and she went back to the window. The room was at the back of the house and the window faced up over the hill. She scanned the hillside for some sign of habitation, but could see nothing; it was open ground covered in gorse, heather and gritty grey outcrops of rock. There were no buildings in sight, and despondently Rosanne turned away from the window once more.

She sat down on the edge of one of the beds to decide what to do next. She stared round the room for inspiration, but none came. Perhaps she could escape through the door as Malley opened it when he came to fetch her, but she knew he would be ready for such a break, hadn't he said he would have someone else with him, Brian someone? He must have been the other man on the boat.

'Now think again,' she commanded herself, and she looked at the room more carefully. The only furniture in it was an old wardrobe with a cracked mirror and the iron beds. A single light socket dangled from the ceiling but there was no bulb. She stared at it all for a while and then an idea suddenly came to her.

'Of course!' she cried, 'Why on earth didn't I think of it before?' And she stripped the two quilts from the beds and knotted them together. It was not easy and she had difficulty in tying a secure enough knot; one that would not slip, but at last she managed by knotting two corners together so that she had the diagonal width of both quilts as her rope. Then she looked round for something to which she could make it fast. There were only the beds, so she tied one end round the leg of the bed by the window and poised herself to let the rest of it down the outside of the house. First, however, she leant out as far as she dare to see if there were any windows immediately beneath hers from which she might be seen, but as far as she could tell there were none. So, she let the rope slip out between her fingers, slithering over the sill until its full length had gone, then she peered out after it. Poor Rosanne could have screamed with disappointment at what she saw. The quilt rope was far too short. If she dared to use it she would end up dangling two storeys above the ground; so much of the length was wasted in knots and the distance from the bedstead to the windowsill. Almost crying with frustration, Rosanne dragged the bed as close to the window as it would go, but it made little difference to the drop at the other end. Dejectedly she hauled the quilts back up and dumped them in a heap on the bed and stared at them in despair. Then she had another idea, and with excited fingers she worked at the knots, to untie the quilts again. As soon as she had separated them she tore at the edge of one, trying to rip it in two so that she would have double the length. The material was old and tore easily and soon she had four lengths of quilt. She joined them again and once more let the rope out of the window. This time it reached within ten feet of the ground and Rosanne felt she could manage to drop the last bit.

She climbed up on to the windowsill and looked down into the garden below. The daylight was beginning to fade into dusk, and a breeze had sprung up that stirred the snake of rope hanging down the side of the house. It was a long way to the ground and Rosanne clutched the makeshift rope tightly to steady herself as she tried to summon up the courage to start her descent. As she pulled on the rope to get a good grip before lowering herself over the sill she heard a noise, a sickening, tearing sound, and she felt the rope give a little. She clutched at the window-frame once more and grasping frantically with her fingertips managed to fling herself back inside; panting heavily her heart pumping with fear, she collapsed on the floor.

It took her several moments to regain command of herself, but when her head had stopped spinning she knelt on the floor to inspect the rope. Where the quilt was knotted round the leg of the bed, the material was so old and worn that at the slightest strain it had begun to rip. She realized that if she had trusted her full weight to the makeshift rope she would have ended up lying on the terrace far below with a broken neck.

'Oh God!' she cried in earnest prayer, 'what am I to do?' And she buried her head in her arms in despair. 'Brendan! Oh, Brendan, I wish you were here.'

The thought of Brendan somewhere not far away, coming to find her, may be already at the cottage, gave her courage once more and she pulled herself together and reviewed her situation.

'I will get out,' she said. 'Now if I can't really escape perhaps I can make them think I have. I must hide somewhere. If they come to get me and I'm not here they'll think I've gone down my bedspread rope, and with luck they won't lock the door again and I can slip out when they've gone.' It was a forlorn hope, but Rosanne needed something to hold on to and so she set her mind to develop this idea.

First, she looked round the room for somewhere to hide and her heart sank once more. There was nowhere that was not so obvious that it could not be checked easily before the men would believe she had really slipped down the rope to freedom. Apart from the old wardrobe and the beds the room was bare, offering no safe hiding-place. She opened the wardrobe door. It was empty except for a few wire coat-hangers, and there was plenty of room for her to curl up inside, but she knew it was no good trying to hide in there, it was the first place Malley and his friend would look when they discovered her missing; and supposing she locked herself in and could not get out again, Rosanne shuddered at the claustro-phobic thought and dismissing the wardrobe from her plans, looked round for another solution. The two beds offered no concealment and for a momen Rosanne felt entirely at a loss. Then the glimmering of an idea came to her.

'I can't climb down,' she thought, 'but I might climb up. If I could scramble up on to the roof there might be another way down.' She turned her attention to the window again and hoisting herself up on to the sill and resolutely refusing to look down, she sat on the ledge, her legs still inside the room and looked upwards towards the ridge of the roof. Above the window the slope of the roof was shallow and instead of the eaves jutting out above the walls of the house the slope ended against a low parapet, which ran the length of the house. Remembering the rectangular aspect of the house she had noticed at the front, Rosanne realized that this parapet ran right round the roof and would make an attempt to escape upwards fractionally safer.

It was the discovery of this protecting wall that decided her. She drew a deep breath and said, 'It's up or nothing.' She glanced back into the deceptive safety of the little attic bedroom and wondered what more she could do to save herself.

'If there's no other way down I'm still trapped,' she thought, pausing again before committing herself to the climb. 'But even so I might hide up there until they've gone and then climb back in.' Encouraged a little by this thought she again prepared herself for the terrifying climb and again paused to consider another problem which now occurred to her.

'How will I know when they've been? If I'm far enough away so that they don't see me I may not hear them. Oh, Brendan, what would you do?'

'I'd make it as tough for them as possible,' she seemed to hear him say, and looked round again to see how she could put his imagined advice into practice.

'Of course,' she cried slithering back into the room. 'Block the door.' She considered one of the beds, but decided it could be shoved aside too easily and she could not use both as her rope was tied to the leg of the one nearest the window. The wardrobe! That was the answer if she could shift it alone; she only had to heave it along the wall a few feet and it would slide in front of the door. Bracing herself against one side of it she put her back against it and, straining with the effort, managed to move the old cupboard a few inches. She paused for breath and heaved again, winning a few more inches. Gradually she moved it inch by inch across the bare floorboards until it stood fair and square across the doorway. Panting from her exertions Rosanne looked at it triumphantly.

'Did it!' she breathed. 'It won't keep you bastards out for ever, but at least I'll hear you coming if I'm stuck up on that roof.'

Flushed and dishevelled she returned to the window. The dusk was gathering outside and she knew she must make her attempt on the roof before the darkness became complete and made it too dangerous an enterprise.

Taking her courage in both hands, Rosanne hoisted herself on to the windowsill once more and holding fast to the casement window which jutted out beside her, eased herself up on to her feet so that she was standing on the ledge and able to see over the white parapet. Cautiously she put one hand over the top and holding tightly to the window with the other, she felt for a handhold of some kind, but there was nothing to grip, no unevenness or crack in the structure, just the smooth face of the parapet and the sloping slates of the roof. Slowly she transferred her second hand from the window to the top of the little wall above her, then with both elbows hooked over the top she began to haul herself up and, scrabbling frantically with her feet trying get some purchase on the open window, she managed to get herself high enough to struggle over the parapet and collapse in comparative safety on the other side. Her heart was pounding, her limbs were shaking and she was terrified, but she had made it. The stiffness in the hinges of the casement window had allowed her to use that window as a stepping-stone and she was free of the room.

For several moments Rosanne lay against the parapet, her burning face pressed against the cool slates of the roof, her body completely beyond her control, never wanting to move again; then gradually she stopped shaking and with a supreme effort she forced herself to move, for from the depths of her mind the warning kept repeating itself, 'You're not safe yet, you're not safe yet.' If Malley should take it into his head to stand up on the windowsill and look across the roof, his face would only be inches away. She eased herself up on to the roof and still resolutely keeping her eyes from the drop below her, scrambled over the slates until she reached the ridge and sat astride it, her back pressed firmly against a chimney-stack. She could smell the wood smoke drifting into the evening air above her and realized that far below her, straight down through the house, was the library where perhaps Paul still sat entirely unconcerned by the fate he had planned for her.

From her vantage-point Rosanne peered through the dusk to see if there was any other way down the roof. As far as she could tell there was none, and unwilling to trust herself over the slates in the near-darkness, she decided to stay where she was, in comparative safety, until she heard Malley trying to break into the attic-room below. She leaned back against the chimney and made a conscious effort to relax, her body at first still rigid, gradually eased and her mind moved from her present predicament to its automatic resting-place, Brendan. She had no doubt now as to how she felt about him. She ached to feel his arms round her, to hear his voice saying her name, to see the humour that lurked behind his dark eyes. The arguments with which she had deceived herself before, her job, her life in London, now faded into insignificance as she accepted the fact that a future without Brendan would be insupportable.

'And yet,' she reminded herself, 'I've no real reason to think he wants me at all — just that one 'darling', and she clung to it now as she faced the possibility that she might never see him again.

It was growing cooler and Rosanne shivered as she waited in the dark up on the roof of Inchmore House. She could see out both sides of the house and, apart from a few specks of light from the village, the darkness around was unrelieved. If Paul Hennessy was still in the house below the windows must be curtained, for there were no shafts of light into the garden.

Suddenly the chill of the night air was overtaken by a chill of horror as another possibility struck Rosanne.

Suppose Malley shut the window. Suppose he believed she had escaped down the rope of quilts and so closed the window before he left the room to go after her. The night afforded her some measure of safety now, but in broad daylight they would easily find her She closed her mind to the possibility, 'There's nothing I can do about it,' she thought firmly, 'So I won't think about it any more.' And she concentrated on trying to place the cottage in the blackness down the hillside.

The minutes dragged by and suddenly that darkness was pierced by two beams of light; flashing and dipping. A car. There was a car coming up what must be the lane to the cottage. Rosanne strained her eyes, watching the headlamps and then saw them go off. A few moments later other lights appeared and she realized that someone was in the cottage.

'Is it Brendan or Ruth?' she wondered, but at that moment she heard the sound she had been waiting for, down below was a bang and then a heavy and continuous pounding. Malley was trying to move the wardrobe. Immediately Rosanne crawled over the ridge, and crouching on the far side of the chimney-stack, sheltered by its darker shadow, she peeped over the ridge of the roof, hoping to discover what happened in the room below.

The banging continued for several minutes, followed by a moment's silence which seemed to Rosanne to stretch into eternity, then there was more noise and a tremendous crash coupled with the sound of breaking glass echoed on the night air, and she realized that in forcing the door open Malley must have tipped the wardrobe over shattering its mirror as he did so. Rosanne could hear the men's boots on the attic floor and the sound of voices, though she was unable to distinguish what was said. She remembered that there was no bulb in the bedroom lamp and realized that the men only had light from the landing and possibly torches to help them search. From her hiding-place she saw the beam of a strong torch probe the darkness as one of them men shone it out through the window, and she heard him say, 'It almost reaches the ground, come on, Brian.'

Their feet thudded back to the landing and gradually the sound died away, leaving Rosanne alone in the silent darkness of the roof, her heart racing and her knuckles white where her fingers gripped the ridge and chimney-stack.

14

It took Rosanne only moments to clamber across the roof to the edge of the parapet above the window. Trembling, she peered over the top and with relief saw the casement still standing wide below her. Climbing back it proved to be easier than climbing out had been. She paused for a moment to compose herself and then gingerly lowered herself over the edge, clutching the open window with one hand and feeling for the windowsill with her feet. As soon as her feet were firm she slithered inside, landing as quietly as she could on the bare floorboards. As she waited for a second to regain her breath, she heard voice in the garden below and knew that Malley and Brian had gone to the bottom of the rope to try and pick up her trail. She drew back from the window hastily in case they should shine the torch upward and almost at once a beam of light swung across the window. Rosanne shuddered in horror as she realized that if she had taken any longer they would have discovered her hanging from the roof three storeys above the terrace.

'No time to lose,' she thought, 'I must get out of here.' And she crossed the room lightly, clambered over the fallen wardrobe, and slipped out through the door. The landing light was still burning and she crept along to the top of the staircase. Hearing nothing from below she ventured down on to the first landing, which was in semi-darkness, lit only by the light from the front hall. There was a thick carpet and Rosanne moved silently to the top of the next staircase. She peered cautiously over the banisters into the hall below. As far as she could see, all the doors which opened into it were closed, including the library where she had sat with Paul. The quiet was complete except for the steady tick of the grandfather clock. She could see the front door with its huge bolts still drawn across and wondered first how long it would take her to drag them back and open the heavy door and second how much noise the bolts and the door would make. Perhaps she would do better to try to slip out through the kitchen. She considered this for a minute but decided against it.

'If I go that way I may not find the way out easily and could well bump into Malley coming back. There's no one here now, it's got to be the front.'

Having made the decision she wasted no more time but crept down the huge staircase into the panelled hall, and across to the front door. As she reached it the silence around her was shattered by the clanging of a loud bell above the door itself. Someone on the outside was ringing to come in. Panic-stricken, Rosanne looked round wildly for somewhere to hide and as she heard movement coming from the library and realized Paul was on his way to answer the bell, she dived beneath the old hall table and crouched there, completely hidden by the chenille cloth that covered it. She was not a moment too soon, for the library door opened and Paul Hennessy crossed the hall and unbolted the front door. Rosanne could not see who had come and feared it might be Malley or Brian to tell him she had escaped, but Paul's voice was raised in welcome and he said, 'Brendan, my dear chap What a surprise! Do come in.'

'Thank you.' Brendan stepped into the hall and Rosanne heard the door close behind him.

It took all the self-control she possessed to stop herself rushing out from under the table to the safety of Brendan's arms. She ached to get to him and warn him, so that she no longer had to face the danger alone, but she remembered the evil-looking gun which Paul had, perhaps even now in his pocket and she stayed where she was, crouching in the semi-darkness hidden by the heavy chenille cloth.

Brendan spoke again.

'Sorry to disturb you at this hour, Paul, but I wondered if Rosanne was here.'

'Rosanne?' Paul sounded surprised. 'No, she's not here. Should she be?'

'No, well, I don't think so,' replied Brendan, 'but she's not at the cottage, no one is, and I wondered if they'd come up here for a drink or something. I know you asked them before.'

'Afraid not,' said Paul apologetically. 'Though I can help you about Ruth and the children. Apparently Ruth's husband rang and said he was arriving at Cork airport early this evening. They all went off to meet him. Aren't they back yet?' he added innocently.

'No,' said Brendan, 'they're not. There must be some delay. Didn't Rosanne go too?'

'No,' said Paul, 'I saw her in your garden earlier as I walked up the hill. We had a brief chat and she asked if she could borrow my rowing-boat. Said something about looking in lobster-pots. I didn't follow what exactly but I said she was welcome to the boat.'

'What time was that?' asked Brendan.

'Oh, I don't know, between six and seven, I suppose,' answered Paul casually. 'Time for a drink? Just a quick one?' He moved towards the library, but Brendan said, 'No, thank you. Perhaps she took your boat straight away; she's probably down at the beach still. The moon's up and she's an incorrigible romantic. I think I'll wander down there.'

'Well, suit yourself,' said Paul. 'I expect she's down there or even back in the cottage by now. I hope she hasn't had an accident with my boat,' he added as an afterthought.

'So do I,' said Brendan darkly and though Rosanne was unable to see his face she could visualize the black expression which would accompany that tone.

'Do go,' she prayed silently, 'Get out of the house before he finds out I've

223

escaped.' And with all her strength she willed him to leave, but he was still in the hall.

'Oh,' said Brendan suddenly, 'do you mind if I borrow your phone to call the airport for news? Mine seems to be out of order, I tried to ring you before I came up.'

Paul crossed to the phone on his desk and picking up the receiver put it to his ear.

'Sorry,' he said, replacing the receiver firmly in its cradle, 'no dialling tone. Mine must be out of order too, probably a fault on the cable.'

'Probably,' agreed Brendan and turned back towards the front door. 'She didn't come up here first?'

'No.'

'Well, thanks, anyway.'

'Hope you do find her all right,' said Paul as he opened the door for his guest. 'Goodnight.'

Rosanne just heard Brendan's return 'Goodnight' before the heavy front door swung to and clicked shut. Paul dragged the bolts across and returned to the library and it was too late. All through the conversation Rosanne had been on the verge of rushing out from her hiding-place and claiming Brendan's protection, but the thought of the gun held her back. Obviously Paul did not know yet that she was free and as he was armed then it was probable that both she and Brendan would have been caught, which would help nobody. So, though longing to go to Brendan, she had not moved and was pleased he had refused Paul's drink and gone directly to look for her; that would keep him safely out of the way until she could escape to him and explain the whole situation.

She heard Paul return to the library but she did not hear him close the door. Very cautiously Rosanne lifted a corner of the thick tablecloth and peeped out. The library door was still open wide and Paul was standing with his back to her, lost in thought, but she was certain that if she tried to creep away now, the movement would catch his eye and she would be seen. So, she decided to sit it out patiently under the table until the way was clear for her to make her break.

She had only waited a few moments when there was a noise from the kitchen and Sean Malley and Brian strode into the hall. Paul swung round at the noise and surprised to see them said abruptly, 'Well?'

'We've lost the girl,' replied Sean Malley equally abruptly. 'We went up to collect her and take her down to the boat, and when we got there she'd gone.'

'How the hell did she get out of there?' demanded Paul angrily.

'Made herself a rope, didn't she? Out of the counterpanes. Climbed out of the window.'

'Fool!' exploded Paul, his anger so fierce that even in her hiding-place Rosanne trembled at the force of it. 'Did you not see the counterpane on the bed?'

'Never crossed my mind,' admitted Sean, and added grudgingly, 'She's a bold girl.'

'Well, that leaves things in a fine state,' said Paul. 'You'd better find her, and fast. Check O'Neill's cottage first. He's been here. I sent him off to the beach to look for her. Don't let them meet.'

'Right,' said Malley. 'Come on, Brian.'

'Did you deal with the dinghy?' Paul called after them.

'We did that earlier, and the cottage phone.'

'Good,' said Paul. 'Well, find that girl and let's get out of here. It's time we were away.'

Malley unbolted the front door and he and Brian disappeared out into the night. Paul went back into the library, closing the door behind him and Rosanne heard the ting of the telephone.

'He was lying to Brendan about the phone too,' thought Rosanne as she hurriedly scrambled out of her hiding-place. Realizing that this was her chance to escape she headed for the back door. She had no wish to meet Malley or Brian in their search for her and the sooner she was away from the hall the safer she would feel.

The kitchen was in darkness and Rosanne moved across it slowly with her arms outstretched in front of her, desperately afraid that she would bump into something and alert Paul. However, she reached the back door without mishap and eased it open. Stumbling down the back steps into the yard below she rushed blindly away from the house, anxious to get as far as possible before Malley and Brian came back. Once she had reached the garden wall and scrambled over it, she moved on steadily up the hill through the heather and gorse, careless now of the noise she was making until she came to a large outcrop of rock where she collapsed in relief at being safely away from Inchmore House, Paul Hennessy and his friends at last. She lay still for a while to collect her thoughts.

'I must find Brendan,' she decided, 'but I must keep away from the cottage.' She tried to picture the landscape as she knew it, to work out which was the easiest way to seek safety and get help.

Rosanne was about to set off soon towards the main part of the village when she heard a noise behind her. Before she could turn or run strong arms twisted one arm behind her and pinioned the other to her body. She opened her mouth to scream but the sound died on her lips as she heard a familiar voice mutter ferociously, 'Don't move or I'll break your arm.'

'Brendan,' she whispered fiercely, 'Let go!' You're hurting me.'

'Rosy? Rosanne Is that you?' The vice-like grip was released and a torch was flashed momentarily on her face.

'Oh, Rosanne, thank God!' and the flashlight clattered to the ground as he gathered her into his arms and held her so tightly that she could hardly breathe. He could not see her face in the darkness, but his lips sought hers greedily, kissing every part of her face until at last they found her mouth. It was a long moment before he raised his head and whispered, 'My little love, are you all right?'

Rosanne clung to him, overwhelmed by his kisses and never wanting to leave the circle of his arms.

'I'm all right now,' she breathed.

Brendan said, 'Thank God!' again and kissed her again, more gently this time, smoothing her hair.

The moon sailed out from behind a cloud and the hillside and the house below it were clearly lit. Brendan dragged Rosanne back into the sheltering shadow of the rocky outcrop and demanded, 'Now, will you tell me what's been going on?'

Rosanne nestled against him as they sat against the rocks and told him the events of the evening. When he heard how she had scaled the roof to escape, his arm tightened round her and he murmured, 'My brave darling,' but otherwise he heard her without interruption. When she had finally described her flight through the kitchen and over the garden wall, she said, 'But I thought you were going to the beach. What miracle brought you up here?'

'Well,' explained Brendan, 'When I got home and you weren't there, and no one was there, I was worried. There was no message and I couldn't believe you'd have gone without leaving one. I thought you must be out somewhere with Ruth, but I couldn't think where you all might be, I mean it was far too late for the children to be out, as a rule.'

'I did try to leave you a note,' said Rosanne, 'I said I should to Paul, but he said it was only for a quick drink and if we saw lights come on before I was back we'd phone at once.'

'And you believed him?' Brendan's voice was slightly mocking.

'I had no reason not to,' said

Rosanne defensively. 'I didn't know what time you were arriving, but you'd implied it would be late and I'd been alone too long; my imagination was beginning to work overtime, every sound made me nervous. So, I was glad of the company. David's flight was diverted to Shannon, and I didn't know when Ruth would be home either.'

'I know, I know,' soothed Brendan, 'but I didn't know then that there even was a flight. I thought you were safely with Ruth. I heard about that from Paul when I came up to Inchmore. He told me you hadn't been there, to his house. I knew he was lying and I wanted to know why, so I decided to wait around and see what happened when he thought I was safely out of the way on the beach.'

'How did you know he was lying?' asked Rosanne, surprised. 'I was listening too, under my table, and he sounded most convincing to me.'

'He would have to me, but for one thing,' said Brendan, 'I could smell your perfume. I knew you had been there recently.'

Rosanne giggled at that. 'I didn't know you had such a discerning nose.' Brendan pulled her closer to him and said with mock seriousness, 'Where you're concerned I'm extremely discerning.' He kissed the hand he held in his and then he went on, 'Now we must decide what we are going to do next.'

'Well, Paul's leaving, I think,' said Rosanne. 'He said something about joining the *Queenie Q* tonight, and that it was time to get out. Brendan, what is going on?'

'Haven't a clue,' replied Brendan, 'but its obviously something shady, and Paul's involved up to the neck. It must be something pretty big too, probably drugs or arms; it's clear he's smuggling something and it must be important if he's prepared to kill you on the off-chance you might have seen something.'

Rosanne shuddered and said, 'He's a very frightening man; he's quite ruthless. I hope he doesn't get away with it.'

'He won't,' said Brendan grimly, 'We must do what we can to make sure he doesn't.' We haven't much time,' he went on, 'we must get hold of the Garda and tell them what's happened.'

'Supposing they don't believe us,' said Rosanne. 'I don't think they really believed me before.'

'We must convince them,' said Brendan, firmly. 'We must at last make them investigate.'

'But they'll be too late,' objected Rosanne. 'Paul was leaving as soon as he could.'

'Then we must hurry,' said Brendan. 'I think we should keep well clear of the cottage,' he went on, 'which means we can't get my car.' He thought for a moment and then said, 'I swore to myself I'd never let you out of my sight again, but I think we're going to have to split up.' He tightened his grip on Rosanne's hand and said, 'Can you find Garda Murphy's house, do you think?

It's a white cottage beyond the church on the far side of the village, overlooking the harbour.'

Rosanne nodded in the darkness, the moon had again disappeared behind a bank of thick cloud and she was unable to see Brendan's face, but she said, 'I think so.'

'Well, go across the hill here and you'll come to a track. It'll lead you down into the village behind the post office, without taking you anywhere near our cottage. It you go quietly, not like an elephant through the undergrowth as you did just now, you should get there all right.'

Rosanne could hear the twinkle in his voice even though she could not see it in his eyes as he referred to her dash from Inchmore House and from the safety of his encircling arm she was able to return the smile and said again, 'I'll find it, but what are you going to do?'

'When you get there make them come down to the strand. I'm sure that's where Paul will go from. He has a little motorboat there and a dinghy. I expect he'll meet up with a fishing-boat which'll take him out to this other ship.'

'The *Queenie Q*?'

'Yes, the *Queenie Q*. He won't risk being seen to board the fishing-boat down at the quay — too many inquisitive eyes. While you get the Garda to the beach as quickly as you can and I'll do all I can to stop him getting away.'

'You mean you're going down to the beach alone?'

'I must. If he once gets aboard that boat waiting out there, he's away.'

'But Brendan, he's armed.'

He heard the fear in Rosanne's voice and said gently, 'I know. I'll be careful, but I've the element of surprise on my side.' Rosanne was not convinced and said, 'But he thinks you're down on the beach, looking for me.'

'I know, but he doesn't know I know about him; and I've quite a score to settle with him if it comes to that.' He spoke grimly and Rosanne knew it was no good trying to deter him. The moon emerged from the clouds for a moment or two and a glance at Brendan's face convinced her. He caught her glance and the harsh look vanished as he smiled down at her.

'We must go as soon as the moon goes in again,' he said softly. 'Just get help to the beach as soon as you can; then when it's all over we must talk to each other properly, there's so much I want to tell you.'

Rosanne opened her mouth to question, but at that moment the moon disappeared into the clouds once more and Brendan jerked her to her feet.

'Now!' he whispered urgently, 'And take care!'

15

Rosanne stumbled across the hillside, trying to move quickly, yet with Brendan's warning in mind, as quietly as possible. It was difficult to find the way in the darkness though her eyes were by now well accustomed to the night and she was at least able to discern the darker shapes of clumps of gorse and rocky outcrops looming against the sky. Even so her arms were soon scratched and bleeding from unseen thorns and though her legs were protected to some extent by the denim of her jeans, hidden stones and boulders threatened to sprain her ankle if she did not slow her pace a little. Terrified at the thought of being stranded on the dark hillside for the night with a broken ankle and at the mercy of anyone out to find her, she slowed down and moved more steadily towards the track leading into Kilbannon.

Below her were the lights of the village and when the moon suddenly sailed clear of its blanket of cloud and she could see better, she discovered she had almost reached the track Brendan had described. She clambered over a drystone wall and dropped down on to the rutted track on the other side. The going was easier now and though she was afraid she would be easily visible in the moonlight, it did mean she could move more quickly. She kept in the shadow of the wall as far as possible as she hurried down towards the village, hoping to slip through and reach the Garda's unseen.

As Brendan had told her, the little track emerged between the post office and the neighbouring cottage on to the main street which ran through the village to the harbour. Rosanne stopped for a moment, sheltering in the shadow of the buildings, and looked cautiously up and down the street. It was poorly lit by only two street-lamps, but she could see one or two parked cars and a well-lit telephone-box opposite the post office; otherwise the street was deserted. She was about to set off down the road when an idea came to her, a better idea perhaps then going the length of the village to find Garda Murphy. It was so simple and saved so much time that she wondered that she or Brendan had not considered it before. They knew the phone at the cottage was out of order, Brendan had tried it and Malley told Paul he had dealt with it, but what was to stop her from using the public call-box? There it was in front of her, the public telephone box and if she slipped into it and dialled 999 things would probably move a lot faster than if she spent time trying to find Garda Murphy's house and then more time convincing him that something was wrong and he must act at once. The more she considered the idea the better she liked it. Once she had made the call she would be able to go to the strand herself to help Brendan. The thought of him there by himself to face an armed and ruthless Paul Hennessy made her heart lurch; and though she had no idea how she could help she knew she could not leave Brendan alone.

It was this that decided her and she darted out across the empty street and heaved open the heavy door of the phone-box. A light burned inside and it did not take a moment for her to snatch off the receiver and dial 999. It seemed an age before anyone answered and when she did the operator spoke slowly and clearly, asking which service was required.

'Police!' Rosanne cut her short and trying to speak calmly added 'As quickly as you can, please.' She glanced out anxiously through the glass sides of the phone box, peering into the dimly lit street, feeling herself very conspicuous in the brightly lit booth, but as far as she could tell all was quiet outside and the street still deserted.

As soon as her call was answered, Rosanne began to pour out what was going on to the policeman at the other end, but he cut through her torrent of words with an abrupt 'Name, please.'

Rosanne Charlton. You must come please now, they're getting away and . . . '

The voice cut in again.

'Where are you speaking from, please?'

'Where? Oh, Kilbannon post office, the call-box.' Rosanne had lost track of what she had been saying and said testily, 'Kilbannon Strand. You must send help or they'll get away to the boat . . . '

'What boat?' interrupted the voice.

'The *Queenie Q*, they're leaving tonight, now because of you searching the lobster-pots.'

The voice sounded bewildered. 'Let's start again, m'am; who is leaving and what have lobster-pots to do with it?'

Rosanne was exasperated and she cried out, 'Do hurry or they'll kill . . . ' The telephone-box door opened behind her and the draught made her spin round as Malley's hand chopped down on the side of her neck and she collapsed forward, crashing her forehead against the coinbox. The receiver clattered from her hand and dangled, spinning on the end of its wire. An anxious, disembodied voice continued saying, 'Are you there, caller? Is everything all right? Caller? Caller?' long after Malley had left the kiosk, for, without troubling to replace the receiver, Malley dragged the unconscious Rosanne out of the brightness of the phone-box, across the road into the shadows at the side of the post office. He had no idea of how much Rosanne had been able to say before he had interrupted her and he knew he had to move fast. At that moment Brian came loping down the street. Malley called him over and between them they supported Rosanne down the street to the harbour. The quay was in darkness except for one light at the far end, shining on the steps which led to the water. Keeping well clear of this patch of light, the two men manhandled Rosanne over the edge into a dinghy moored to a ring in the sea-wall; and while Malley sat ready to deal with her should she come round, Brian rowed swiftly, noiselessly out to the little fishing-boat riding at a mooring in the concealing darkness of the harbour. Minutes later they were nosing out from behind the inner harbour wall into the wider expanse of the bay and heading out to sea.

* * *

When Rosanne came to, a few minutes later, she found herself lying on a hard, heaving floor that stank of old fish. For a moment she had no idea where she could be and scarcely cared, so strong was the throb in her head and the ache in her neck. She felt desperately sick and fought the rising waves of nausea. At length they subsided and clutching her head she tried to decide where she was and how she came to be there. Gradually, despite the ache, her brain began to function and she realized she must have been taken aboard the fishing-boat. She remembered being in the phone-box and turning to find Malley at the door, and fought a moment to remember what she had been doing there. Then it all came flooding back to her and she realized that once more she was a prisoner and this time she was in even more danger, for her captors already had her aboard the fishing-boat and she did not doubt they would tip her unceremoniously overboard some time between now and the rendezvous with the *Queenie Q* out at sea.

The wheelhouse door opened and Rosanne heard footsteps on the deck. Quickly she closed her eyes and let her head loll back into the uncomfortable position from which she had raised it. Though her eyes were shut she felt the man looking at her and fought to keep herself limp and still. She heard him call, ' 'Twas one hell of a blow you hit her, Sean, she's still out.'

Rosanne could not hear the words of Sean Malley's reply, but Brian continued, 'Should I tie her up? We don't want her causing more trouble.'

'Don't tie me,' she prayed silently. 'God, please don't let them tie me or I'll never live until tomorrow.'

Sean replied to Brian's question, but again she could only catch a few words . . . 'Hennessy . . . later . . . unconscious.' And then she heard Brian coming closer. He bent over her and she could smell him, a mixture of stale sweat and fish, his breath warm on her cheek as he peered at her. He lifted one of her hands and let it go so that it flopped back on the deck, bruising her knuckles. However, she managed to display no sign of consciousness, and Brian, apparently satisfied that she was still out cold, stumped away without bothering to tie her up.

Rosanne immediately realized that her chance of survival depended on her being able to convince her captors that she was still unconscious until an opportunity to escape arose. She lay back against the bulwark where she had been dumped by Malley and shivered, for although this provided some shelter, the breeze freshened as they crept out to sea. She still felt very queasy, but whether it was due to the motion of the boat or the blow Malley had dealt her in the telephone-box, she did not know. Trying to ignore her sickness, Rosanne looked round cautiously; she wanted to see if there was anything which might help her in her bid to escape. The lamp in the wheelhouse farther forward gave her a little light though her part of the deck was in shadow, but occasionally the moon sailed free of the clouds and enabled her to see her surroundings, though at first they seemed to yield little which might help her. She was hampered by the intermittence of the moonlight and by her need to remain as still as possible lest any movement attract the notice of the two men. Then she saw it, lying on the deck beside a coil of rope. At first she could not believe her eyes, and peered again to be sure she was not mistaken, but there it was, a wooden-handled gutting-knife, its blade honed narrow and razor-sharp, glinting in the moonlight, gleaming as if it were trying to take her eye.

It was further along the deck and Rosanne could not reach it without moving. She spent an agonizing moment deciding what to do.

'If only I could get hold of that,' she thought, 'I'd have more of a chance, especially if they decide to tie me up.'

She glanced up at the lighted wheelhouse, both men were staring out to sea, neither was paying any attention to her, so praying that they would not look round, Rosanne eased herself to her hands and knees and crawled towards the knife. In seconds it was in her grasp and she was back in the position she had been before. She slipped the wicked-looking knife into the top of her jeans under her sweater, and smiled to herself nervously, 'I mustn't bend over too quickly or I shall gut myself,' she thought. But though the knife was dangerously placed, she could think of nowhere else to put it where it would escape a cursory inspection and yet be to hand if she needed it, and the feel of it there was very comforting.

Rosanne shut her eyes and waited, her mind resting on Brendan. A stab of fear went through her as she thought of him alone on the dark beach, waiting for Paul Hennessy.

'Please God, let him be all right.' She shivered with cold and the knot of fear remained in her stomach. Even so she dozed, and when she jerked awake she certainly had no idea of how much time had elapsed, or what had woken her so suddenly. Then she realized there was silence. The boat's engines had ceased, the throbbing vibrations were still and the wheelhouse light was out; the little fishing-vessel drifted on the tide and the only sound to be heard was the rhythmic slapping of the water against the hull. Rosanne could not see Malley or Brian, but she could hear their voices up in the bows of the boat. She wondered if now was the time to try to escape, but she had no idea where they were, how far from land, how far from help, and she realized it would be suicide to slip over the side into the cold, unfriendly waters of the sea. Then she heard another sound which made her heart sink and almost decided her to take her chance in the sea. It was the sound of an outboard engine and it was coming fast. Rosanne had no doubt it was Paul Hennessy coming to join Malley and Brian on the fishing-boat. That was why they had stopped; that was why they were drifting, they were waiting for Paul to come.

Her two captors heard the boat, too, and came round the side of the boat to catch the line Paul threw them and make it fast so he could come aboard. As he appeared over the side, Rosanne closed her eyes hastily and lolled her head as it had been when Brian had examined her before. For a moment Paul did not see her and he shouted orders to Sean Malley.

'Get under way fast, Sean, I've had trouble on the strand and we may have unwanted company before long.'

Brendan! Rosanne knew at once that it was Brendan who had caused the trouble on the beach; but was he all right? Paul was here and in foul mood. Had he left Brendan dead on the strand?

The fishing-boat's engines juddered to life again and then settled to a steady throb as they carried the boat out towards the ship waiting in the darkness. Then Malley drew Paul's attention to Rosanne and she could feel his eyes boring into her.

'Why haven't you tied her?' he snapped.

'Ah, she's still out cold,' replied Brian amiably. 'Sean hit her too hard.'

'Well, she won't be for long,' said

Paul. 'She's caused enough trouble as it is; we've had to wrap up the operation in this area because of her. Tie her up now and we'll deal with her when we reach the *Queenie Q*.'

'Right you are, boss,' said Brian and collecting a length of rope approached Rosanne.

Determined that if her hands had to be tied at all they should be in front of her so she could still reach her knife, Rosanne had arranged them casually in her lap and Brian, thinking her still unconscious, grabbed her wrists in one of his great paws and bound them swiftly with the rope, leaving them secured in front of her. Rosanne rejoiced inside as she felt him do this, but her heart missed a beat when she heard Paul call down, 'Search her too, Brian.' For a moment she thought she had lost her knife, but Brian replied, 'I've done that already, sir. We did that as soon as we got her on board. She's got no weapon.'

Paul appeared satisfied with this and

Brian left her tied on the deck and went to join the others. Immediately Rosanne set to work to ease the knife from its hiding-place. It was more difficult than she had anticipated, but at last she got it free and, gripping the handle between her knees, gently rubbed her bonds against the blade. At first she thought she was making no impression, but then she felt one strand loosen and moments later she was free.

All three men were in the wheel-house, none of them paying any attention to her. The engines were roaring again and the little fishing-boat was heading steadily out to sea. Rosanne knew that now was her chance to escape and as it might be the only one, she had to take advantage of it at once. She considered her action quickly. Could she slip over the side into Paul's boat without them seeing or hearing her? She decided it was unlikely because at the speed they were now travelling the little boat being towed along behind would be at the fullest extent of its painter, the line that held it to the fishing-boat. It would take too long to haul it close alongside and difficult to keep it there as she tried to drop into it. If she went into the water herself she would have a better chance of clambering aboard, but she realized that she must cut the boat free first or it would be dragged out of her reach before she could get into it. If she was really lucky and the three men did not see her go she might drift for a while until it was safe for her to start the outboard and steer the little boat for home and Brendan. Rosanne felt a surge of hope run through her; for the first time since she had come to her senses to find herself captive on the fishing-boat, she felt really optimistic about her chances of escape. She glanced once more at the wheelhouse and then made her move.

Slowly and quietly and clutching her knife firmly in her hand, she edged her way over to where the line from Paul's boat was tied. With one slash she cut it adrift and then easing herself over the side of the fishing-boat, slipped into the sea. It was cold enough to make her gasp, but she wasted no time and struck out away from the fishing-smack to where the little motorboat bobbed, a dark shape on the dark water.

She reached it safely, but found it quite a struggle to clamber aboard from below it. Puffing and panting she heaved herself upwards and managed to slither in head first, flopping on to the bottom of the boat, where she fought to get her breath back. Incongruously she remembered the mackerel Brendan had caught flapping helplessly on the floor of the boat gasping its life away, and for a fleeting moment she renewed her sympathy with it, then she jerked herself back to the present and its dangers.

She sat up cautiously and looked across at the receding stern of the fishing-boat still chugging away from her out to sea, leaving a swirling trail of white water behind it. Suddenly she heard an angry shout and saw the wheelhouse door fly open. Two figures rushed out, one towards the place where she had been, the other to hold up the severed line which had been towing Paul's boat.

Realizing the danger was not over even yet, Rosanne cowered in the bottom of the boat and prayed she was not visible from the fishing-smack. She heard the note of the engine change and peeped over the side of the boat. The fishing-boat was circling as if coming back to look for her and Rosanne knew she must do something or she would be recaptured. Unconcerned now as to whether they saw her or not, she turned her attention to the powerful outboard which Paul had swung clear of the water over the stern of the boat before he climbed up on to the fishing-boat. Rosanne struggled to get it into the water, and having succeeded made herself calm down and remember the instructions Brendan had given her. This engine was not the same as his and it was difficult in the darkness to see how it worked. She found the petrol switch and the throttle, but then she realized with a sinking heart there was no ignition key. Paul must have taken it with him, automatically taken it out as one would a car key.

At that moment the capricious moon sailed clear of the clouds and flooded the sea with light, revealing Rosanne clearly to the searchers in the fishing-boat. She could not escape. Then she saw the oars lying in the bottom of the boat; her mind told her there was no way rowing would help her, but even so she scrabbled frantically, hooking the dangling rowlocks into their rests and heaving the oars out to set them in the rowlocks. But even as the fishing-smack turned towards her, there was a shout from one of the men aboard and Rosanne could see him, a black shape in the moonlight, pointing back towards the way they had come. Immediately the fishing-boat altered course once more, turned tail and went full speed ahead out to sea.

Rosanne strained her eyes in the direction he had pointed and there, across the water she saw a powerful launch, speeding towards them over the waves, bouncing across the surface like a pebble expertly skimmed from the beach. At first she thought it merely in pursuit of the fast retreating fishing-boat, and was afraid she would be left to drift unnoticed. She leapt to her feet, waving and shouting and to her joy the power-boat veered sharply and swept up beside her bobbing craft.

Willing hands reached out to haul her aboard while others took the little motorboat in tow. As she scrambled to safety she was aware there were several men on board before her attention was claimed by one of them. Brendan. With a joyful sob she collapsed into his arms and clung to him as the pent up emotion of the last forty-eight hours exploded within her and she wept, shaking uncontrollably. Brendan held her close and let her cry, rocking her gently as he would a frightened child waking from a nightmare.

'It's all right, it's all right,' he soothed and gradually Rosanne's sobs died away. Safe within his arms at last she smiled wanly through her tears.

'Sorry,' she said. 'It must be shock, I suppose.'

'Shock at seeing me?' Brendan teased, settling her more comfortably against him.

The power-boat swung round in a large circle and set off at a more sedate pace back towards Kilbannon. Rosanne suddenly realized what was happening.

'They're getting away,' she cried and clutched urgently at Brendan's arm. 'Paul and the others are on that boat. They're getting away. There's another ship out there to meet them.'

Brendan smiled down at her. 'You're right,' he said. 'But it isn't the one they're expecting. There's a fishery protection vessel out there which will arrest them and bring them back before they reach the safety of international waters.'

'But weren't you chasing them?' demanded Rosanne.

Brendan shook his head. 'No,' he said simply, 'I was chasing you.'

'Me!' cries Rosanne incredulously, 'How did you know I was there?' She shivered suddenly as the night air cut through her wet clothes.

'I'll tell you everything when we're safely at home and you've had a hot bath. Just thank the lifeboat station for sending their inshore rescue-boat so fast when your message got through.' And despite her protests he refused to be drawn on the subject any further, he just stripped off his thick sweater and pulled it over her head and then holding her to him again warmed her with his own body until they reached the harbour once more.

16

The Garda was waiting on the quayside with a car and immediately they were safely ashore Brendan and Rosanne were whisked back to the cottage. Despite Brendan's sweater Rosanne was shivering and he insisted that before she did any explaining or made any statements she should be allowed time for a hot bath and to find warm dry clothes.

There was no sign of Ruth, David and the children.

'David must have been so late that they decided to stay overnight in Cork,' said Brendan. 'I expect they'll be here first thing in the morning.'

'Do you think Ruth's been trying to phone,' asked Rosanne wearily.

'Probably, but she knows I'm here, so she won't worry too much about it being out of order,' replied Brendan.

'Now, let's get you dried out before you catch pneumonia.'

Rosanne was grateful that Brendan was there to take charge and she meekly obeyed his instructions to go up at once and get out of her wet clothes while he drew her bath. She sniffed as she crossed the landing, wondering what it was she could smell, then she realized and called down to Brendan, 'Take the casserole out of the oven, it must be quite dried up.' How long it seemed since she had set it to cook, a lifetime ago, yet only a few hours.

'All right, I'll see to it,' Brendan called back, 'Now do go and have your bath.'

Obediently Rosanne stepped into the steaming bath and emersed herself thankfully in the water, submerging completely so that even the top of her head grew warm and the sea-salt soaked out of her hair. Brendan had left a large glass on the end of the bath and as the warmth gradually began to seep back into her she sat up a little, reached out for it and tasted the drink. It was brandy and as it coursed down inside her she felt its warmth spreading with fiery fingers and she lay back in the water, clutching the glass and revelling in the luxury of being alive and safe and warm. She allowed her mind to wander back across the evening, but she kept returning to the moment which dominated her mind, Brendan's kisses on the hillside. As she remembered their warmth she felt a thrill run through her and as she remembered how warmly she had returned them she felt weak in case he did not feel about her as she was beginning to dare to believe he did.

Suddenly the bath seemed too hot and Rosanne felt faint with its heat. She struggled to her feet and climbed out, groping for the towel on the rail and wrapping it tightly round her. The faintness passed and, setting it down to neat brandy on a completely empty stomach, she hurriedly dried and dressed in dry corduroy trousers and a warm pink sweater. She towelled her hair and then combed it straight and with it still clinging damply to her neck went downstairs to join Brendan and the waiting policeman.

As she came into the room both men got up and Brendan led her to the fire which was burning cheerfully in the grate.

'You were quick,' he said as she curled up in the chair at the fireside.

'Well,' said Rosanne, 'I didn't want to keep the police waiting.' She looked across at the man who had driven them up from the harbour; she had never seen him before. He smiled his appreciation as he got out his notebook from his pocket. He was not in uniform and Rosanne wondered if he was indeed a policeman. However, he introduced himself as Superintendent Donnelly from Special Branch in Cork, and then began to ask questions.

'Perhaps, Miss Charlton, you would be good enough to tell me again what happened two nights ago while you were out fishing?' He smiled encouragingly and Rosanne embarked once more on her story. When she had finished he said, 'You're quite sure there were packets of some sort in the bottom of the keep-box?'

Rosanne nodded. 'Quite sure,' she said, 'and rolls of some sort too.'

'Like rolled up pictures, for instance?' asked Donnelly.

'Yes, just like that.' As she answered Rosanne suddenly realized what Donnelly was getting at.

'You mean Paul Hennessy . . . ? They were the ones stolen from Paul Hennessy?' she gasped.

Donnelly shrugged. 'Hard to say,' he said, 'but possible, even probable.'

'But it was Paul Hennessy's man, Sean Malley, who tried to run me down.'

'He was just the courier, come to collect whatever Hennessy had left him. Probably when he saw you peering into the very lobster-box that he was supposed to take with him he panicked.'

'He did not seem the panicky sort,' said Rosanne with a shudder. 'He was cold and calculating.'

'Even so,' said Brendan, coming into the conversation for the first time, 'it must have thrown him to find you there.'

'But I still don't understand what was going on,' complained Rosanne. 'What was so important that they would kill me if they thought I'd discovered it?'

'Several things,' replied Donnelly. 'Paul Hennessy ran as organization which would export, or import illegally, anything anyone wanted brought in or out.'

'He's a smuggler,' said Rosanne.

'Well, yes, in a way, but he smuggled into and out of the country.'

'But what?' Rosanne was still puzzled.

'Anything which would make him money. Recently there have been several robberies from the bigger houses up and down this coast, and none of the things as been traced. I expect much of the easily identifiable stuff went out of Ireland, courtesy of Paul Hennessy.'

'But what about his own house?' asked Rosanne. 'Why burgle that?'

'Could be one of several reasons,' answered Donnelly. 'Maybe he thought it the ideal way of having the pictures and the insurance money and he just couldn't resist the chance of making some easy money; or maybe he thought it would look strange if his collection, well known locally as it was, was not touched, and he did it to throw us off the scent. Either way, it was you spotting the rolls which alerted us. We knew something like this was going on in this area, but we'd been unable to pinpoint where.'

'We said it was strange the burglars should do his house while he was here and not while it was empty,' remarked Brendan.

'Yes, we thought so too,' agreed Donnelly.

'So,' said Rosanne 'He took his own

pictures and things and wrapped them in waterproof and then while pottering innocently about in the bay left them quietly in the box.'

'That's right,' said Donnelly. 'Then Malley would collect them on the way out to sea and pass them on to some ship waiting outside Irish waters.'

'And it worked in reverse for things coming in,' said Brendan.

'Exactly,' said Donnelly.

'What kind of things?' asked Rosanne.

'Anything easily transportable which would make money. Drugs, small arms, jewellery; anything anyone wanted moved in or out secretly. I've no doubt he had plenty of clients, but nothing was ever found when there were spot checks on the fishing-boats about to sail. Of course, no one queried fishermen checking lobster-pots, it was too routine to excite comment.'

'But who is Paul Hennessy really, then?' asked Rosanne.

'Lives in Dublin and is apparently a legitimate antique dealer, though we've had our eyes on him for some time; he bought Inchmore House as a holiday home to give him an excuse to be down here when he needed to be.'

'What about his wife?' said Rosanne remembering the move Paul had made when they were alone in the library at Inchmore House.

'Hasn't got one,' replied Donnelly.

'Well, he brought someone down who was said to be his wife,' said Brendan.

'Part of his cover of respectability in this area. She helped to establish him as a quiet married man who loved to escape from the bustle of Dublin and spend his time fishing and walking. You stumbling on his smuggling system threatened his whole organization.'

Rosanne nodded at this and said, 'When he came on to the fishing-boat he said it was due to me that he was going to have to close down operations round here.'

'We needed to flush him out,' said Donnelly. 'We hoped a little excited activity in the bay yesterday might force him to make a move, and it certainly did.'

'Jeopardizing Rosanne's life as a result,' said Brendan, his expression darkening.

'Indeed, as it turned out,' agreed Superintendent Donnelly, 'And for that we sincerely apologize; we should have studied the man's reactions more closely. I thank God Miss Charlton is safe.'

'It's certainly no thanks to you,' said Brendan ominously.

Rosanne said, 'I'm safe, and it was worth it to catch Paul and the others, don't you think?'

Brendan seemed to accept this, for he turned to her and said, 'Tell us what happened after you left me. You were going to find the Garda, how did you come to be on that fishing-boat?'

Rosanne settled herself more comfortably in the chair and described what had happened. When she reached the part about the phone-box, Donnelly said, 'When you were grabbed by Malley we had no idea what had happened, so we sent several cars to the village. You certainly got things moving.'

Rosanne continued her story until she got to Paul Hennessy's arrival.

'He said he'd had some trouble on the beach,' she said turning to Brendan. 'I was afraid it had been with you.'

'It was,' said Brendan grimly.

'What happened? I was afraid he'd killed you.'

'Well, he might have,' admitted Brendan. 'He came down to the strand soon after I got there. I hadn't gone there directly in case our friends were looking for me. I went across the headland and approached from the other way. I was just checking the boats drawn up on the sand when he arrived. It was dark and though I'd been listening for him I didn't hear him, he must have moved like a cat. Anyway, I had found a line tied to a ring in the wall and remembered then that Paul sometimes leaves his boat moored in the bay on a long line if the weather is fair and I was just hauling in on this when he jumped me.' He smiled across at Rosanne reassuringly.

'He hit me with something and down I went. I must have been stunned for a moment or two, for the next thing I knew he was hauling in his boat. This time it was my turn to surprise him and I launched myself at him and we both ended up scuffling in the sand, but his first blow must have affected me more than I realized, for he soon shook me off and before I could gather myself he'd drawn a gun on me.' Brendan gave a harsh laugh as he went on, 'He made me pull the boat ashore at gunpoint and keeping me covered he got clear. No glory for me, I'm afraid.'

'He might have killed you,' cried Rosanne with deep concern, 'Are you badly hurt? You didn't say you were hurt.'

'Just a bit bruised,' Brendan reassured her.

'And you came to rescue me,' she almost whispered.

'When we arrived, Mr O'Neill was alone on the beach and seemed very glad to see us,' put in Superintendent Donnelly.

'Until I realized you weren't with them,' said Brendan. 'I asked where you were and no one knew so then I asked them how they knew where to come. When I heard about the phone-call, broken off in the middle and the receiver left dangling, I guessed Malley had found you.'

'Luckily, we were able to call out the inshore rescue-boat,' said Donnelly, 'Or we might have been too late.'

'Not too late to save Rosanne,' said Brendan proudly. 'She'd rescued herself already.'

Rosanne blushed rosily at his praise and avoided his eye. For something to say she turned to the superintendent.

'Will Paul Hennessy get away?'

'Not unless he's prepared to take on the Navy,' Donnelly replied. 'The fishing-boat was intercepted and they were all arrested before they made contact with the *Queenie Q*. He stood up and slipped his notebook in his pocket. 'I've got most of this,' he said, 'But we'd like a formal statement in the morning. Perhaps you'd bring Miss Charlton into town tomorrow some time,' he went on, turning to Brendan, 'When she's rested and recovered from her ordeal.' He smiled down at Rosanne, who suddenly felt too tired to get up from her chair, and said, 'Goodnight, Miss Charlton, we'll see you some time tomorrow.'

As Brendan saw the superintendent to the door and locked it behind him, Rosanne swung her legs down and resting her elbows on her knees and her chin on her hands stared into the dying fire. No one had made it up while they had been talking and the leaping flames had died away to a dull glow as the last log smouldered gently to ash. It was over, all the excitement and the fear of the night were gone, and Rosanne felt utterly exhausted.

'Shall I ever feel like me again?' she wondered and for a moment tried to imagine herself back at school, facing a class of twelve-year-olds, but the whole idea was too remote to be visualized, and she gave up.

The living-room door shut behind Brendan with a click and without a word he crossed the room and knelt beside Rosanne's chair. Very gently he took her hands in his and as she looked into his face she saw such tenderness in his eyes that it brought unexpected tears to her own.

'Darling,' he whispered. 'Darling, don't cry. It's all over now. I'm here to look after you.'

She buried her face in his shoulder and his arms slipped round her and he held her close, murmuring soothingly into her hair. Then very gently he put her away from him and sat back on the floor and looked at her seriously.

'Rosy, he said, and she was surprised at his use of her shortened name, for he had seldom used it, 'Rosy, do you love me?'

'That's not fair,' said Rosanne with something of her old spark, 'That's not a fair question.'

Brendan looked surprised. 'Why not? You know I love you.'

Rosanne looked confused and colour flooded her face, making her look even more adorable to Brendan, and all she could say was a faint 'Oh.' Then collecting her wits together a little, added, 'You never said so.' Brendan smiled and said huskily, 'What did you think I was saying when I found you on the hillside? Oh, my love, don't look at me like that or I won't be responsible for what might happen.' He moved to take her in his arms once more, but Rosanne held him away, determined now was the time for the question that had worried her for so long to be answered once and for all. She said softly, 'What about Mary, Brendan?'

A frown creased his forehead and he answered irritably, 'What about Mary?

Ruth told you she's marrying someone else and I hope she'll be very happy. I haven't seen her since before you came to Ireland.'

Rosanne's heart sank as she realized that he was not being honest with her. She knew from their phone call that Brendan had been with Mary. With her heart breaking at his deceit she looked away from him, then clutching the rags of her pride round her she faced him again and said stiffly, 'That's not true, Brendan. I heard you speaking to her the other day when we were on the phone.'

Brendan stared at her for a moment still frowning and then he began to laugh and his laughter hurt her to the core.

'It's not funny,' she snapped, 'I might have lived with the memory of Mary if you had been honest about it.'

Brendan was immediately contrite and said quietly, 'No, I know, and I'm not laughing at you. Let's get this clear once and for all, this business of Mary.

Ruth told you that I was in love with Mary, right?' Rosanne nodded. 'Well, I admit we were very close, but I never told her I loved her and I never asked her to marry me. I did love her in a way, I suppose, but I didn't want to spend the rest of my life with her. She hoped, I think, that I'd change my mind, but when I didn't she finally left me and said everything was finished between us. I was pretty upset, though even then I could see that the blow was to my masculine pride rather than my heart.' He grinned wryly as he added, 'I'm afraid I have rather a lot of pride and I don't take kindly to having it trampled.'

Rosanne opened her mouth to ask again about the conversation she had overheard on the phone, but Brendan laid a finger on her lips and said, 'Let me finish,' so she closed her lips again and waited.

'All this happened in the spring and I haven't seen Mary since. She's found someone else now and she's getting married in a month or so; as I said, I hope she'll be very happy. Now, when I rang you the other day it was from the lab where I work. I told you I was doing some research. I have a lab assistant; her name is Mary. I must have spoken to her. I don't know any other Marys and if I knew a hundred it would make no difference, I wouldn't be interested in any of them. Now,' he spoke with mock severity to make her smile, 'is there anything else you'd like to know?'

Rosanne, however, did not smile. She was cold and pale, ashamed at her doubts of Brendan; she wanted to escape his gaze, to be alone, but Brendan ignored the change in her, took hold of her hands once again and very softly repeated his question.

'Do you love me, Rosy.'

She felt his hands tighten on hers until their grip hurt her as he waited for her answer. She looked up into his eyes and said, 'I love you, Brendan.'

'Say it again.' His voice was still soft but his eyes commanded.

'I love you, Brendan.' And as she said it she realized just how much. He stood up and pulled her out of her chair and into his arms, but it was she who pulled his face down to hers to kiss and kiss again.

After a few moments Brendan dropped into the big armchair and drew Rosanne on to his knee so that he could hold her closely, and she nestled against him.

'Tell me when you knew what you felt,' she demanded when she was comfortable. 'Was it only tonight?'

Brendan smiled. 'No, I've known for days, ever since you and the children were cut off by the tide and I thought for a while you had drowned.

'You were very angry with me that day,' said Rosanne tentatively.

'Because I was afraid, afraid for all of you, I thought I'd lost you almost before I'd found you. But you saved the children and I was so relieved to find you it made me angry; and then I realized why.

'Why didn't you tell me?'

'Well, for a start there was George to be considered. I thought you were in love with him.'

'Never like I love you,' said Rosanne softly and she felt Brendan's arms tighten round her as if he was still afraid she might disappear and he said with great satisfaction, 'Good. That takes care of George.'

'I'm going to London,' he said after a while.

'What?' Rosanne was startled.

'The company's sending me to London for a year or two. That's what I was going to tell you, but it was only definite yesterday. So, you won't have to give up your job.'

'Give up my job?'

'Well, not at first, anyway. When we have children it'll be different.'

'Brendan . . . ' began Rosanne and then stopped as he looked at her with the old familiar irritatingly mocking expression.

'Well,' he said 'That's if you'll marry

me.' Then he said, 'Will you?' There was fleeting anxiety in his face as he asked and he added like a child remembering its manners, 'Please?'

Rosanne looked at his beloved face and her heart seemed to explode with love for him as she answered gently, 'Yes, Brendan,' and added with a twinkle, 'Please.'

The dawn crept over the hillside and a dull grey light invaded the cottage. Rosanne noticed the grey square of the window and said, 'It's morning, Brendan. It's getting light. Ruth and David'll be here soon.'

Brendan glanced out of the window. 'It's raining,' he said. Rosanne laughed, for to her the world was glowing and golden.

'Rubbish,' she cried, ' 'tis just a fine soft Irish morning.'

We do hope that you have enjoyed reading this large print book.

Did you know that all of our titles are available for purchase?

We publish a wide range of high quality large print books including:
**Romances, Mysteries, Classics
General Fiction
Non Fiction and Westerns**

Special interest titles available in large print are:
**The Little Oxford Dictionary
Music Book, Song Book
Hymn Book, Service Book**

Also available from us courtesy of Oxford University Press:
**Young Readers' Dictionary
(large print edition)
Young Readers' Thesaurus
(large print edition)**

For further information or a free brochure, please contact us at:
**Ulverscroft Large Print Books Ltd.,
The Green, Bradgate Road, Anstey,
Leicester, LE7 7FU, England.
Tel:** (00 44) **0116 236 4325**
Fax: (00 44) **0116 234 0205**

THE SOARING HEART

Heather Pardoe

Menna Williams is a talented woman, determined to make her own way in a male-dominated world. When she becomes house-keeper at Bryn Hyfryd, Menna has grander dreams in mind and, with the help of the dashing Tal Lloyd, it seems they will become reality. But Tal's younger brother, Rhodri, is constantly warning Menna about Tal's reckless nature. Gwenan Lloyd, mistress of Bryn Hyfryd, has problems of her own to overcome. Which of her two nephews, Tal or Rhodri, should she trust?

LOVE'S LOST TREASURE

Joyce Johnson

When Rosie Treloar discovers her fiancé is an unscrupulous conman, she flees London for her native Cornwall. Here, she takes a job as a tourist guide and meets American Ben Goodman, who is researching the mystery of his family's legacy, lost during the English Civil War. Rosie, increasingly attracted to Ben, becomes involved with his mission, unaware that there are other sinister forces seeking the legacy — forces which could threaten her newfound happiness with Ben . . .

THE MARRIAGE INHERITANCE

Michelle Styles

When Caroline Adams arrives at
Rafe Worthington's Northumber-
land castle, she finds her holiday
cottage is uninhabitable. Rafe offers
her accommodation in return for
playing his fiancée, to foil his
scheming cousin Jenna's plans for
the castle. Caroline agrees, but then
she confesses all to Rafe's great
aunt. Jenna's scheming is exposed
and Caroline runs back to London,
but Rafe follows her, prepared to
give up the castle for the woman he
loves.

THE MARRIAGE BARGAIN

Lisa Andrews

When Elinor is forced to marry William de Valences, it is for her lands, not her beauty. But King Henry makes it a condition of marriage that William should provide proof of Guy de Riddington's plotting with the French. William falls in love with his wife, but suspects that squire Robert Latimer is her lover. William rids himself of his rival and keeps his bargain with the king, leaving him and Elinor free to enjoy married life together.

ICE MAIDEN

Catriona McCuaig

On the same day that she's made redundant, Kat Ingram learns that River Farm, their family home for generations, may have to be sold. To top it all, George Logan, from neighbouring Stoneygates Farm, proposes marriage as a way to help save River Farm. Kat decides to visit her sister in Canada, where she meets and falls for wealthy artist Ambrose Legris. When George tries a more romantic approach, Kat must decide — talented, arrogant Ambrose, or safe, dependable George?